REFU

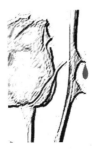

KIRSTY FERRY

www.rosethornpress.co.uk

Refuge

ISBN-13: 978-1479376469

Prologue

Present Day

The wave crashed into the side of the rowing boat, rolling it almost onto its side. The moon was breaking through the clouds, a pale disc illuminating the ragged edges of the dark clouds against the night sky. He pulled on the oars, trying to control the boat and ducked as salt water splashed over the side and soaked him. He strained his eyes, tasting the sea on his lips and peering into the darkness. He could just about make it out – the ghostly, grey box, balanced on four spindly legs rising out of the water. The causeway was covered, invisible under the incessant waves breaking over the surface.

***

A dark figure stood up on the shore of the Island next to the abandoned lime kilns. She looked down onto the beach below. The shale was covered with water now, the waves rushing into the openings in the front of the kilns, crashing and whirling into the caverns inside. She raised her head and saw the poles rising out of the water, leading towards the kilns. Despite the wind blowing in off the sea, she didn't feel cold. She closed her eyes and felt it sweep around her, lifting her dark hair from her shoulders.

She took a step forward. Then another step. Then she stepped neatly off the edge. The waves never broke as her body landed in the ocean and the waves closed over her head.

Present Day

Guy cradled his mug of coffee as he sat in the dining room of the Bed and Breakfast. The remains of a fried breakfast were pushed to one side of him and a newspaper lay open. *Drowning at Lindisfarne* ran the headline. Another body had been washed ashore, the third in as many months. The door to the refuge had been swinging open, slamming into the door frame. The water had reached the top of the steps at high tide: the coastguard thought that maybe the young lad - a backpacker - had opened the door to see how deep the water was. They presumed he'd slipped and fallen into the North Sea and been swept away by the tide.

Guy sighed. He wasn't convinced. The lad's belongings had been left at the hotel. He had nothing with him, not even his mobile phone. Who went out without one of those things nowadays? It seemed to Guy that he had been intending to come back before the tide cut him off. He had plenty of opportunity; the tide tables were well advertised, there was no reason for him to miss the chance of a clear causeway. Suicide? Guy didn't know. He hoped not.

'What do you think about that?' Guy looked up and saw the landlady standing next to him holding the coffee pot. 'The third young lad to die up here recently. It's making us sound like a hotspot for something.' She frowned. 'I don't know what their idea is. You'd think they'd learn from the ones that went before them.' She shook her head. 'More coffee?' Guy nodded and passed his mug over. 'Oh look. You've hardly touched it,' she scolded. 'You need to eat more. You'll waste away.'

Guy smiled. 'I'm fine, really. They're all tourists, aren't they?' he asked. 'Nobody local.'

'Yes, all visitors,' sighed the landlady. 'There's no reason for them to stray off the Island like that. There's plenty of tide tables up. Perhaps they think they can make it back – the posts lead them towards the Island don't they? To the old lime kilns; but they don't reckon on the tides.' She shook her head again. 'Is it putting you off staying?' she asked.

'No, not at all,' said Guy. 'I'm fully intending staying as long as I have to.' He smiled again. 'Don't worry.'

The landlady looked at the young man sitting before her. He had a nice face, she thought; honest and open. She could imagine lots of women melting at that nice smile; he had blue eyes and blonde

4

hair as well. She smiled back at him. He reminded her of a lad she once knew; one of the summer visitors. 'Well, as you said, you've got work to do here haven't you?' she said.

'Yes. A research project,' said Guy. 'Really, I'm not going anywhere.'

'You finished with that, then?' asked the landlady, reaching for the newspaper. 'I'll get it out your way.'

'No, it's OK. Just leave it. Thanks,' said Guy. 'I'm still reading it.'

'Oh, all right,' said the lady and smiled at him. 'Enjoy your day. Dinner's at seven. If you leave the Island, you'll need to be back around four, just to make sure you don't get caught. Don't want you headlining those papers, do we?'

'Not at all,' said Guy. 'I'll be fine.'

***

The mini-bus drove down the incline onto the causeway. The tide was out, but the road was still wet, the tarmac shiny from the waves which had opened it up to the traffic. Lucas tried to ignore the clamour from the back of the coach as his Uni friends threw screwed up paper napkins and takeaway coffee cups at each other. This was supposed to be a history field trip, and he'd already guessed that he'd be one of the only ones treating it that way. He felt the weight of his mobile in his pocket and was conscious of the fact that it was totally silent. Laura hadn't called for weeks. It was a pretty safe assumption that it was definitely over then. He wouldn't delete her number just yet though. Maybe in a week. Or a month. Or even two...

'Hey, Lucas!' shouted Drew, 'if you've decided you need something to help you forget, there might be some nice Island girls here who'll help you.' There was a roar of laughter from the back of the coach. It was clear what they all had on their minds, and it definitely wasn't history. They all seemed strangely excited at being marooned on this island for two nights.

Lucas raised his hand in acknowledgement but didn't turn around. There were more shouts of laughter then someone called out,

'Cool! What's that place for?' The bus lurched as a few lads pushed their way over the other side of the coach to peer out of the window. Drew forced himself in front of Lucas and leaned over him, one hand on Lucas' shoulder.

5

'Get off me!' snapped Lucas. Drew lifted his hand and replaced it on Lucas' head. He ruffled the boy's sandy coloured hair. Lucas smacked him away and Drew laughed.

'Temper, temper,' he said, putting both hands on the window and staring at the white box, which raised up out of the sand and balanced on long, giraffe-like legs. A kind of stepladder led up to the doorway which was firmly closed against the biting wind sweeping in off the sea and buffeting the mini-bus.

'Dunno. I think it's the refuge hut,' said Lucas, following Drew's gaze. 'You're supposed to sit in it when you get caught in the tides.'

'Think they've got a vending machine in there?' asked Drew. 'DVD player? Electric fire? TV? Nah, bet they haven't. Probably full of damp old tourist leaflets and sand.'

'Isn't that where that kid committed suicide?' piped up Alex. 'I saw it in the paper at that service station.'

'Yes! That must be it!' cried Drew. He stared at it in ghoulish fascination as the bus passed it and headed towards the Island. 'Cool,' he said again. He moved Lucas' bag out of the way and dumped it on the floor. He sat down on the empty seat next to his mate. 'Yes, we've got to get you some Island life,' he said, nodding. 'Don't want you to be the fourth one, eh?' he nudged Lucas sharply in the ribs.

'Pack it in,' muttered Lucas, shifting in his seat. He was regretting the confessions that had spilled out in the wake of several pints and being dumped by Laura. Unfortunately, for once, Drew had been a bit more sober than him, and could remember most of the conversation. He'd had great fun tormenting him ever since. Drew was a mate, and solid one at that; but Lucas would hate to have him as an enemy, that was for sure.

'We're he-er...' shouted someone, doing a bad impersonation of the Poltergeist film. Everyone laughed: everyone, that is, except Lucas. He so wasn't in the mood for this.

'Come on, let's get the gear unpacked,' said Drew, nudging him again. He sprang up from his seat and began hauling his baggage from the luggage shelf above their heads. The driver had given up asking them to stay seated and keep their seatbelts fastened, somewhere on the A1. He just made sure he pressed the brake pretty hard: the bus stopped quickly and the lads standing up wobbled a bit. There was an outraged shout as someone's bag hit someone else on the head, and Lucas shrank back in his seat, deciding to wait until the group calmed down enough for him to stand up and get the rest of his luggage.

'I'll go and get our room sorted, mate,' said Drew, bounding down the aisle on long legs. 'That way I can bags the best bed.' He jumped off the bus and Lucas saw him run into the B&B, knocking Alex sideways and laughing about it as Alex hurled abuse after him and gave chase. Lucas sighed. Whatever, he thought, and stood up. He checked his mobile automatically, hoping to see the envelope icon telling him he had a text message from her. The screen was blank and he shoved it back in his pocket. There didn't even seem to be a signal. Brilliant.

Lucas was last to leave the bus. He at least had the courtesy to thank the driver as he stepped onto the Island.

'See you in a couple of days,' said the driver. Lucas slammed the door for him, and the bus pulled away, honking as Lucas raised his hand to the driver. The driver was taking no chances – he obviously wanted to get off that island. He probably didn't fancy being stuck there overnight with Lucas and his friends. Lucas didn't even fancy it much, if he was honest.

Lucas stared around him hoisting his bag onto his shoulder. It suddenly seemed very quiet. There was nothing but the drone of the wind and the shushing of the sea around him. He had the oddest feeling that someone was watching him. He turned quickly and saw a young girl, maybe eighteen, nineteen years old. She was sitting on a fence across the road, her red hair falling in waves to her shoulders. Lucas caught her glance and she smiled at him. One of the Island girls, he presumed, just waiting for a bus load of students to pull up. Her and Drew would get on famously.

'Hello,' she said. 'Are you with the visitors?'

She must be well used to strangers pitching up on the island; it was a small place. She'd know they weren't locals. Well, it cost nothing for him to be polite, he supposed.

'Yes,' he said. 'For two nights.'

'Concise and to the point,' smiled the girl. She hopped off the fence and came over to him. She was petite and skinny with it, but she moved gracefully, just like a dancer. 'I'm Cass,' she said, holding out her hand.

Lucas hesitated for a moment, then took it. 'Lucas,' he said. The girl smiled at him again. Her eyes were a queer sort of azure blue.

They made her pupils look enormously black and her lashes were thick and dark, and framed them perfectly. Most people of that colouring had pale, unremarkable eyelashes, but hers were different. He remembered Laura's dressing table, full of little pots of magic this and special that. She'd go through tubes of mascara, he remembered, piling it on, opening her eyes wide in the mirror and building her lashes up. Her mouth would gape open while she did it, her whole demeanour so full of concentration that he'd laugh at her. He actually quite missed seeing her get ready. She was a welcome sight in the morning. This Cass, whoever she was, didn't look like she'd ever been to a make-up counter in her life. Her skin was a flawless creamy colour, and her cheeks rosy pink, like her lips. She looked fresh and natural – even down to the eyelashes.

'So, two nights?' she asked. 'That's long enough, I guess.'

'Long enough for what?' asked Lucas.

'Long enough for me to get to know you better,' said Cass, tilting her head to one side. 'I'm looking forward to it.' She smiled and turned away from him, heading back to the field. 'Oh,' she threw back over her shoulder, 'the lime kilns. I'd go there if I were you. If you're interested in history, that is. We've got the castle and the Priory and the gardens and things, but nobody seems to give the lime kilns the time of day. You should go.'

Lucas opened his mouth to reply, but she had already turned back and was climbing the fence into the field. He watched after her for a moment, then pushed the door to the B&B open. Cass. Interesting. Quickly, he slapped the thought away. That's what had got him into trouble with Laura.

Kester Lawson had watched his sister die. Her name had been Summer. It suited her – she was golden and bright, like a warm July day. Looking back, Kester was pleased his parents had made them sit for formal photographic portraits. The gentleman had come over from Bath with his new equipment; he would produce ambrotypes, he had told them. They were better than daguerreotypes: but much more expensive, especially if he had to go away and hand-tint them. Kester's parents, always keen to practice the newest fads, and indeed, to be seen to be practising the newest fads, had demanded Kester and Summer's presence for the portraits. There were the usual sets of stiff, family portraits: Kester and his sister standing behind his parents, one of his father standing with his hands on his mother's shoulders, one of Kester and Summer together - his face was slightly blurred in that one – unfortunately, he had moved just at the wrong time.

'It is so typical of you!' Summer had laughed. 'I despair of you. Can't you do anything right?'

The portrait of Summer had been his favourite, although at fourteen, he was loathe to tell her that. The gentleman from Bath had made a perfect job of capturing Summer's peachy skin and long, barley-coloured hair. Sparkling, cornflower blue eyes complimented the rose tinted mouth and there she was, captured forever at sixteen years old. She was going to have a coming-out ball when she was seventeen, her parents declared. The picture would be pride of place in the ballroom, subtly located so the young men would have to pass it every time they walked towards the door.

Summer never made it to seventeen. It had been the autumn of that year – ironic, really, when Kester thought about it. She had seemed a little more distracted than usual; desperate to ride out every day, yet coming home begging to go to the family house in Grosvenor Square, London – because life was more exciting in London and she now knew people from London.

'May I ride out with you?' Kester had asked one day. It was the beginning of September and the countryside was slipping into one of those long, warm Indian summer afternoons.

His sister had glared at him. 'Why ever would I want you to come with me?' she had snapped. 'Do I need a chaperone? And a fourteen year old boy at that? I think not.' She had stormed out of the drawing room and slammed several doors behind her.

Kester stared open mouthed, then found his voice. 'Who mentioned I had to chaperone you?' he shouted at the closed door. 'What have you got to hide?' He had made it his mission at that point to discover what she was, indeed, hiding.

***

The next day, Kester slipped out of the house and hid in the stables, waiting for Summer to walk around and take her horse out. Peeping out from behind a hay bale, he saw her enter the building. Summer's long skirts swept the slate floors and an elaborate, feathered hat was balanced on her head. She walked up to her usual roan mare and fondled its mane. Kester narrowed his eyes. She didn't usually get that dressed up for riding. He waited until she had mounted the horse and watched her disappear out of the stables, head held high, perched on the horse side-saddle. Kester heard the clip clop of the horse's hooves ring out over the cobbles in the courtyard, the mare speeding up as his sister reached the archway which led into the garden. Giving her a few minutes to get ahead, Kester mounted his horse and kicked it in the flanks. The horse started and trotted out into the courtyard. Kester urged the horse on a little faster and followed Summer through the archway. He could just see her on the horizon, a small, black dot threading through the outskirts of the woods. Summer would have a chaperone that day, whether she liked it or not.

Kester kept his eyes on her, following her at a safe distance until she was swallowed up by the trees. He kicked the horse again and began to gallop after her. There was nowhere to go through the woods, except to an old, disused flour mill. It was a picturesque spot; they had often ridden there with the governess on the pretext of a 'nature lesson'. Kester reined the horse in and wondered if that was the way he should go. It was to the right, just over a little stone bridge. He made up his mind to casually ride by the mill, when a scream rang out from over the bridge. He recognised it at once.

'Summer!' he shouted. The scream started up again and there was a sound of pounding hooves coming closer and closer to him. They rattled over the bridge and Kester saw his sister hurtling straight towards him on the horse. She wasn't wearing her hat, he noticed, and her hair was flying loose behind her. The roan mare bore down on him and he pulled his horse into the undergrowth, not knowing what to do.

'Kester! Dear God, what are you doing here? Please, you have to go. Now! Hurry!' she cried. 'Don't let him find you!'

She sped past him and he called after her. 'Summer! Who is it? I'll fight him for you!' The bravado of a fourteen year old held no sway.

'Just leave!' Summer cried. She turned around, perhaps to shout something more, and that was when it happened. A tree branch cracked Summer across the head, and she was lifted out of her seat. Her long skirts and many petticoats somehow hooked around the horns of the saddle, and Kester watched helplessly as she smacked off the ground and bounced along in the wake of the horse.

Before he could move, a black whirlwind seemed to blow up from the direction of the mill. That was all he could think to describe it as later. Something whipped past him, and he saw an arm reach out and grab hold of the roan mare's bridle. The horse's head was yanked at an awkward angle and it whinnied in pain, but it had the desired effect. It stopped running and Summer lay like a bundle of rags, bloodied and battered on the ground.

'Thank you!' Kester tried to say. His voice cracked and it came out in a whisper. The man – for he seemed like a man; a tall man, dressed all in black with a pristine white ruffle at his throat - ignored him. He knelt down next to Summer and carefully brushed her hair away from her face. Kester thought she was still alive: her chest seemed to be moving slightly. Then the man took hold of a hank of Summer's hair and pulled her head as roughly as he had pulled the horses. He bent over the girl and what Kester saw next sickened him. The man tore at Summer's throat with his teeth and the girl's body jerked. Her back arched and then she flopped down onto the grass as the man continued his work. Kester felt the bile rise in his throat. He couldn't watch any more. He turned the horse and galloped as far away as he could, as fast as he could. Only when he was safely out of the woods and near the house, did he dismount and stumble away towards a dry stone wall, where he vomited until he could vomit no more.

It took him years to realise that he couldn't have saved her then, even if he'd tried. But he swore that one day he would hunt the creature down. And if he couldn't find that one, he would make it his new mission to kill as many of them as he could.

A degree in Theology from Oxford didn't help. Kester thought that it might have enabled him to understand the creature he had seen. The only thing it did, however, was make him worry that Summer's soul was somehow trapped between Heaven and Hell; worse still, that it was in Hell itself. They had given her a Christian burial of course. He remembered standing by the mausoleum in the grounds of the chapel, watching the white coffin being lowered into the building. Nobody had ever been able to explain away Summer's injuries. They put them down to the accident and Kester had never spoken of what he'd seen. A marble angel would eventually grace the mausoleum, sculpted in the image of his sister. He was pleased they had the angel made. And pleased about the ambrotype. Otherwise, all he could have remembered about Summer was the creature leaning over her and the jerking of her body as it drained her blood.

Kester's Theology degree had made him question a lot of things, but fortunately it had also given him access to the great University's library. He spent hours reading through thick, gilt-edged, leather-bound tomes researching the creature. He knew it had it had to be a vampire of some kind – there were many such creatures in folklore, and just as many ways of destroying, or, at least, confusing them. Grains of rice scattered before them to distract them, silver crosses, charmed amulets...the list was endless. One particular item caught his imagination – a fabled silver dagger, studded with diamonds and allegedly blessed by Holy Men in the twelfth century. The whereabouts of the dagger were unknown and rumours abounded about it. Kester traced his forefinger over ancient, yellowing paper, reading and re-reading the information.

The dagger had been lost during the Crusades, the scholars said: taken to the Holy Land in the keeping of the Knights Templar. Part of the Templar's secret initiation ceremony, the scholars implied, was to learn the art of Vampire Slaying. The reason the Templar had been disbanded in 1312 they suggested, was because they were failing to carry out their duties efficiently. The false confessions tortured out of the men during the 1307 arrests in France had nothing to do with the Crusades. It was an elaborate hoax to fool the public – and to hopefully fool any vampires that had been enlightened to the Templar's real purpose in life. The date the French arrest warrants had gone out was significant – Friday, October 13th, 1307. *Dieu n'est pas content, nous avons des ennemis de la foi dans le Royaume - God is not pleased. We have enemies of the faith in the kingdom* – they were told. The scholars had surmised that this was only relevant to the vampire slaying part of the Templars' oath.

Kester sighed. The dagger was obviously lost somewhere abroad; its end as hazy as its beginnings. He closed the book and became aware of whispering behind him in the library.

'Scott's *Marmion*!' said a young man's voice. 'What fool decided to enforce that upon us? I'm inclined to agree with Jeffrey's thoughts in *Edinburgh Review*. The whole poem is flat, tedious and a vehicle for Scott's historical knowledge. It's a damned shame I have to read this. Listen.' He began to quote from the poem. 'This is the man droning about Lindisfarne:

> *Dry-shod, o'er sands, twice every day,*
> *The pilgrims to the shrine find way;*
> *Twice every day, the waves efface*
> *Of staves and sandalled feet the trace...'*

Kester caught his breath. He knew a little about Lindisfarne. He knew it was located off the Northumbrian coast and deemed a place of pilgrimage. He also knew there was a Priory on it and that the lime merchant, William Nicoll from Dundee, was in the process of building some lime kilns up there. Kester's father had written to him, mentioning all sorts of recent industrial achievements. His father still hoped Kester would opt for a more manly career, taking pride in the estate he would eventually own. Kester's father didn't know it, but Kester planned to sell the house and estate once his parents were no longer alive. It held nothing for him but those horrific memories of his sister. As he listened to the young man behind him, his gaze was drawn to a sketch of the dagger. The artist had faithfully reproduced all that he knew about it: the dimensions, the number of diamonds on the hilt, the curlicues moulded into the silver handle. Kester stared at the picture, then quietly slipped a small knife out of his waistcoat pocket. With one, neat slice, the page came away in his hand and was transferred into his pocket. He envisaged a trip to London rather soon. Then maybe a trip up to Lindisfarne – to Holy Island. If the dagger could have been produced once, who was to say it could not be replicated? He had plenty of money – surely, a jeweller of some note could not refuse a young man such a request? He would have to consider carrying out some sort of blessing at Holy Island, perhaps. And after all, was it not possible that a Theology student might want

13

to make a sort of pilgrimage up there? Really, it was all going to be surprisingly simple when he thought about it logically.

***

Kester pushed open the door to the jeweller's workshop in Clerkenwell. The door creaked on its hinges, and Kester found himself in a small room, devoid of human occupants. The only sound emanated from a clock on the mantelpiece and a ginger cat gazed listlessly at him from in front of the fireplace. Kester moved towards the counter and tried to see into the back rooms. The cat unfurled itself and padded through the dividing door, waving its tail elegantly in the air as it moved.

'Good morning!' Kester tried. 'Is anybody here?' No response. He cleared his throat and raised his voice. 'I say, gentlemen! Is there anybody here?' Silence. 'I have a commission for you – this may work to your advantage...'

A moment passed, and the dividing door opened slightly wider. The cat slunk back through and resumed its office at the fireplace. Kester allowed himself a small smile. Between them, the cat and Kester had clearly caught someone's attention.

'Hello?' he said again. The door opened further and a small, dark man appeared. He wore round glasses and a dark suit. This, then, decided Kester, must be Mr Goldschmidt. A very appropriate name and one which was emblazoned above the shop window outside.

'Good morning,' the man said. 'Can I help you, Sir?' His heavy accent seemed to be European.

'Mr Goldschmidt?' Kester asked.

'Solomon Goldschmidt at your service,' said the man. He bowed slightly.

'My name is Kester Lawson. Mr Goldschmidt, I wonder whether you would be able to help me? I'm looking for someone who can make me a copy of this.' He took the paper out of his frock coat pocket and unfolded it. He pushed it across the counter and Mr Goldschmidt leaned over the picture, pushing his spectacles back on his nose.

'Oy, oy, oy!' he spluttered. 'What do you mean by this young man?' He stepped back from the counter and stared at Kester. 'Do you know what this is?'

'I do, Sir,' said Kester. 'The original is missing, I believe: therefore I would like a copy.' He stared back at the jeweller.

14

Solomon Goldschmidt sucked his breath in. 'This dagger you show me, young man. It was used by highly skilled individuals. This area of London is drenched in Templar blood. Our Priory has links to the Knights Hospitallers, a religious order founded by The Blessed Gerard to provide medical assistance during the Crusades – I myself was party to certain instructions when I set up my business here. The Priory may now be part of St John's church, but the crypts still remain...'

'Sir,' interrupted Kester. 'I really do not think I need a history lesson from you. I have asked you to do a job for me. You will be well paid. What is the problem?'

'Forgive me, Sir, but you have not been trained in the ways of the Knights Templar. You cannot hope to utilise this item correctly, Sir.'

'Who said I was going to use it?' asked Kester. 'Can I not simply have a replica of this item because I appreciate the workmanship? Because I want to display it at my family home?'

The jeweller was silent for a moment. He looked at Kester, trying, it seemed, to read the hidden meaning behind the bland words. Eventually, seeing no way of breaking the young man's façade, he relented. 'Very well, Sir,' Goldschmidt said quietly, shaking his head. 'I cannot turn away trade, I am not a rich man and do not have the luxury of choosing my clients and refusing work. Therefore, I will do as you bid.'

'Excellent.' Kester drew the paper towards him again. He stared at it, memorising it. 'I suppose you will want to keep this. I must request, however, that it is returned to me with the finished product.'

'Of course, Sir,' bowed the little man. 'I shall aim to have it ready in two weeks.'

'Two weeks?' asked Kester. 'Are you certain about that? I was hoping for it a little more quickly.'

'Two weeks,' reiterated Goldschmidt. 'Even that is generous. There is an incredible amount of work to be done on it: the curlicues alone, Sir, not to mention the diamonds. The materials all need to be sourced and crafted...'

'Very well,' said Kester. 'I can see there is nothing else to discuss.'

'Except the price, Sir,' the jeweller reminded him.

'The price is no object,' said Kester. He unfolded another piece of paper and handed it to the man. 'That, Sir, is the maximum I am willing to pay. I trust that will suffice.'

The jeweller's eyes widened as he read the figures. He bowed again. 'Young Sir is very anxious to have his decorative dagger,' he said.

'Yes, I am. I shall see you in two weeks,' said Kester. 'Please ensure it is ready for me.' He bowed slightly to the jeweller and turned on his heel. He left the shop, and stepped out onto the bustling streets of Clerkenwell. 'Templar blood, indeed,' he muttered to himself. There was only one sort of blood he intended to see the streets running with. Then he thought for a moment. Did vampires bleed? Probably not. He shook his head and turned towards St John's church. While he was here, he may as well take a look at it. If he sat quietly enough in the church, God might give him the strength and the wisdom to avenge his beloved sister.

***

Two weeks to the day, Kester returned to the jeweller's. This time, Solomon Goldschmidt was sitting at the counter, concentrating on polishing up a pocket watch. He lifted his head as the door opened and smiled at Kester.

'Welcome back, Sir,' he said. 'I trust you are well?'

'I will feel better when I see that my request has been complied with,' Kester answered. 'Am I to be disappointed, Mr Goldschmidt, or is it ready?'

'It is ready, Sir,' said the jeweller. He left his seat at the counter and went through the door into the back rooms. Within a few moments, he returned, clutching an object wrapped in soft, black velvet. He placed it on the counter and reverently unfolded the coverings. Kester, hardened as he was against the world and emotionless to everything except his drive to avenge Summer, could not stop his eyes widening at the sight of the dagger.

A small sound escaped his lips. 'It is beautiful,' he whispered, 'perfect, in fact.' Kester reached out and ran his fingertips over the curlicues, feeling the smooth silver shapes undulating beneath them. Golden light from the small fire in the room caressed the blade and reflected back a hundredfold in the immaculately cut diamonds studding the hilt. 'How much?' he asked, unable to tear his gaze away.

16

'Ah, Sir, it is a work of art. It took me so long to make. It is from the heart, Sir, from the heart. I am afraid it cost, well, it cost more, but I am happy to accept the maximum you offered me...' said the jeweller.

Kester was vaguely aware of the tremble in the man's voice as he chanced his arm on the bill. 'Take it, Goldschmidt,' he said, throwing a bundle of notes onto the counter. 'It is yours. You have earned it.' Kester picked the dagger up and weighed it in his hands. He curled his fingers around the hilt and swung it through the air. It made a barely audible whoosh. He brought the dagger down in a stabbing movement and he smiled. 'Perfect,' he repeated and wrapped the dagger up in the velvet. 'Thank you for your assistance.' Goldschmidt nodded and smiled, and Kester turned to leave the shop. The door opened as he reached it, and he stood to one side to let a young woman walk in. She looked up at Kester and smiled her thanks. Kester bowed and left the shop, his precious package held close to his chest. It was only when he was halfway down the street, that he realised he had left the original engraving of the dagger behind.

'Damn!' he muttered, and turned back. He had expressly asked for that picture back. Well, he couldn't blame the jeweller, he supposed. He had given him the dagger and it was Kester who had left after that. No matter, he would go back and retrieve it. But first of all, he ducked into an alleyway and paused for a moment. He pulled a small bottle of Holy Water out of his pocket, gathered from the font in St John's church two weeks ago. He was going to Lindisfarne, no question about it. The dagger needed to be blessed properly at the Priory, but this would suffice in the meantime. He made the sign of the cross and closed his eyes, bowing his head. He murmured the Lord's Prayer over the dagger and sprinkled the Holy Water onto it. Whether it would work or not, he did not know, but he felt the strength and determination grow from within him. He could do this. He could avenge Summer.

**

'Good morning, young lady,' smiled Solomon Goldschmidt, addressing the girl who had walked into his shop as Kester left. 'And how am I to assist you today?'

The young woman smiled. She was very pretty. She had hazel eyes and fair hair, parted in the middle and knotted neatly at the nape of her neck. A small bonnet with violets pinned to it was

17

perched on her head, and she wore an elegant violet-sprigged crinoline. She looked charming, Goldschmidt thought. He felt magnanimous; he had made more than enough money from that young man to allow him to live comfortably for several months.

'I am looking for a pocket watch for my Papa,' the girl said. Her voice was faintly accented; French perhaps. Goldschmidt nodded, waiting for her to continue. 'I am told you are the best watchmaker here in Clerkenwell?'

'I do not know of your sources, but I am inclined to agree,' said Goldschmidt.

'I am willing to pay?' said the girl, the words sounding a little like a question, as though she were asking his permission.

'Well, of course!' laughed Goldschmidt.

'Please may I take a look at your work?' asked the girl. 'Please would you advise me what your greatest...how you say it...achievement has been? I love my Papa,' she pouted prettily, 'but he is far away and he is worth every pound I am willing to pay.'

'Aha, I am afraid I cannot show you my greatest work, my dear,' said Goldschmidt, 'as that young gentleman just walked out of my shop with it!'

'How extraordinary!' said the girl. 'Ah, well, I cannot agree to you producing a watch for my Papa if you cannot show me your work.' She shook her head daintily and the violets in her hat wobbled. She dropped a little curtsey. 'Thank you, kind Sir, but I shall leave it for today.' She gathered up her skirts and turned to leave.

'Wait!' cried Goldschmidt. He did not want to lose the chance of a sale. He looked around the room and his eyes settled on the discarded, yellowing page that the Dagger Gentleman had left behind in his haste to leave the workshop. 'Do you see this? This dagger has been recreated perfectly for the gentleman you just saw leave the building.'

The girl paused and half turned. 'Why, Sir! You jest, surely? How can that be? I do not think I can believe that. It is too, too, convenient. Your best work has simply just – gone? With that gentleman? '

'It is true!' cried Goldschmidt. 'See this picture? I swear I have produced the exact same item for that young man.'

The girl turned back and came towards the counter. She held out her hand. 'Please may I see the picture?' she asked.

'Certainly,' said the jeweller, and passed her the engraving. 'A perfect, silver-handled, diamond encrusted dagger. The gentleman was appropriately,' he coughed delicately, 'thankful. I was rewarded well.'

'Interesting,' said the girl. 'You do know what this is, Sir?' she said. Her eyes hardened.

'I...errr..I know it is a decorative silver dagger,' said Goldschmidt.

'You lie, Sir. You know exactly what this is,' hissed the girl, her demeanour changing. She slammed her fist on the counter. 'You made this for him? We thought as much. News travels. Enjoy your reward, Sir.'

The girl launched herself at the jeweller and grabbed him by the throat. She dragged him over the top of the counter, and sunk her teeth into his neck. There was a bloody splutter, and he fell lifeless to the floor. There was a movement behind her and she swung around, just in time to see Kester push the door open. Their eyes locked and Kester paused only for a second. She threw herself at him, but he was quick. He raised his hand and the creature impaled herself on the silver blade. Kester felt the dagger sink into her body, slicing through her strong flesh as if were water. There was an unearthly shriek and the vampire fell to the floor, crumbling into dust.

Kester stood, his heart pounding in his chest, staring at the pile of ash on the floor. His stomach started to churn and he swayed, willing himself not to faint. He had done it. He had killed one of them. His hand shaking, he stumbled across the floor and snatched the sheet with the engraving on from the counter. The picture was a talisman – he was meant to come back for it, meant to kill that creature. He knew then that his Lord had set him on the right path.

**

The trip up to Holy Island had been tedious to say the least. Kester wanted to go at a weekend, particularly on a Sunday, which had made his trip more difficult to organise. He had travelled up from London and was staying in a hotel, high up on the wind bleached Northumbrian coast. This last leg of his journey was by horse and carriage. He had spoken to the hotelier and consulted the tide tables. He knew he had a good few hours on the Island before the tide turned and cut him off from the mainland. The smoke from the lime kilns hazed the island as the carriage took Kester across the causeway. Kester wore a heavy, black cloak, wrapped up well against the gusts of wind which blew across the sea: the folds of the cloak were also an ideal place to conceal the dagger tucked into his waistband. He wanted to urge the driver to move faster, and swallowed his annoyance at the horse which was picking its way carefully along the causeway. Better to arrive safely, he told himself repeatedly, better to arrive safely. The other passenger in the carriage was an official looking gentleman, dressed for business. He carried no baggage, but sat watching the smoke from the kilns. Kester could just make out the wagons carrying carts of coal from the staithes to the kilns, and the wagons full of, he assumed, burnt lime on the way back to the ships which waited by the jetties.

'Wonderful sight, ain't it?' said the carriage driver. 'Good to see the old industry picking up again. Got to be careful though, after that ship blew up a few years ago.' He wheezed out a laugh. 'Aye, 1847. *The William* it were, from Berwick. Never forget that. The old quicklime in the hold set ablaze by the water tha' leaked in. Then they had to wait until the tide came in and did the decent thing – put the flames out, it did. Aye, 'twere a grand sight, that were.' Neither Kester nor the other passenger replied, but it didn't seem to put the old man off. He commenced singing to himself, enjoying the lament of an old Border ballad. Kester wasn't here as a tourist and, as he had told the jeweller in Clerkenwell, he didn't want a history lesson. He shuddered slightly as he remembered the pretty girl in the violet-sprigged dress. The image hardened his resolve to hunt the creatures down and destroy them. His ultimate ambition was to kill the one who attacked his sister, but he knew that was unrealistic. He continued staring at the Island, watching it grow closer and closer as the horse trotted across the causeway.

After some time, the land was firm beneath the horse's hooves and the animal sped up. Kester gripped the side of the carriage as they bumped onto the Island and the man opposite him shifted in his seat, leaning slightly forward as they approached the small town. The carriage driver pulled the horse to a halt and took his payment from his passengers.

'Four hours!' he shouted at them. 'Be here in four hours. That will keep us safe for the journey back.' He doffed his cap and trundled off further into the village leaving the passengers standing by the side of the track.

'Four hours?' said the other passenger. 'Plenty of time.'

20

'Apparently so,' replied Kester. 'Now, if you will excuse me, I must find the Priory. No doubt I will see you on the return journey.'

'No doubt,' said the man. He nodded at Kester and looked around him. Seeming to identify where he needed to be, he headed in the direction of the lime kilns. An inspector of works, Kester assumed. Understandable, especially as these were the new kilns, built to replace the older ones elsewhere on the Island.

Even though the Island was small, there was plenty of life on it. Fishermen wandered out of some of the cottages, heading to the coast to prepare for the tide. There were workers dotted about here and there from the lime kilns and men driving wagons on the roads. Kester soon discovered an inn on the Island. He hurried past it as it rang with laughter and chatter; he wondered vaguely if he would be able to buy some food there later on. Soon, the arch of the ruined Priory loomed over the rooftops and Kester wound his way through the tiny streets. He was acutely aware once more of the dagger he wore on his hip.

Kester reached the Priory and paused for a moment. He looked up at the position of the sun in the sky and judged where the east would be. In the east end of the Priory, he knew he would find what he was looking for: the *piscina* and the *aumbry*. For centuries, the monks of Lindisfarne would have poured unused Holy Water down the *piscina*, ensuring that it fed back into the earth. The *aumbry* would be nearby – a space where the sacrament vessels would have been kept. Kester had decided before he came to the Island where he would go to have the dagger blessed the best way he could. In the absence of monks, he would perform a simple ceremony himself. Water would have collected in the *piscina* over the years – it would hold a trace of whatever was holy. The dagger could be placed in the *aumbry* whilst Kester prayed. It was the best he could do. He stood in the Priory grounds and turned eastwards. Then he began to walk slowly through the ruins, mentally preparing himself.

A strange sort of peace hung over the Priory. Sure enough, Kester found what he was looking for in the ruins of the eastern part of the Priory church. He slipped the dagger into the hole where the *aumbry* had been and knelt before the raised altar of the old Priory church. He felt the spirits of generations of monks settle nearby, as if they had come to join him in his contemplation. Kester was not the first person to make a pilgrimage here and he would not be the last.

21

The resting places of St Aidan and St Cuthbert were well documented and their tombs had originally been built at the Priory. Kester bowed his head and prayed to Aidan and Cuthbert as well as to God, and finally he looked up and gazed at the stone niche which was the site of the *piscina*. He stood, and, taking two small phials from his pocket, he walked over to the wall. He could see that rainwater had collected around the *piscina* and lay in puddles on the shelves of the small stone arches. Kester wrapped the phials in white cotton fabric and laid them on the sacred ground where the blessed water would have flooded out from the hollowed stone. The cloth was a linen handkerchief, a delicately embroidered piece, which had originally belonged to Summer. Kester felt it was appropriate – as virginal and pure as she had been. The cloth also reminded him of his purpose and the fact that he could not allow himself to fail. He murmured prayers as he performed his ritual, and then laid the squares on the shelves. The cloth soaked the moisture up quickly. Kester picked up the handkerchief and squeezed the water into the phials, half filling each one. Then he corked the phials and prayed once more. He wrapped one of them up in the cloth and scratched a hollow out of the ground. He buried the bottle by the Priory wall beneath the *piscina* and covered it up again. If he ever needed more Holy Water, he would know where to come. He moved over to the *aumbry* and took the dagger out of it. Then he sprinkled some of the water from the other bottle onto the blade. It was done. The rest was up to him.

***

Kester checked his pocket watch. He still had a while before the horse and carriage returned and decided to walk towards the lime kilns. He might see the gentleman he had travelled with. Now his task was complete, he could afford to be magnanimous and entertain a conversation with the site inspector.

He heard the screams and shouts before he actually saw what was happening.

'He's gone in! He's gone in!' a man was yelling. 'Into the kilns!'

'What happened?' shouted another.

''Twasn't even the water – twasn't even an explosion! He just went in! He fell!'

Kester began to run. His instinct was to help the men or, at the very least, to try and provide comfort if anyone was beyond help.

He had heard tales of caustic burns from these things, of men being blinded and disfigured. He never thought he would be close enough to almost witness it though.

'Can I help?' he shouted as he pounded across the tracks. The carts and pulleys had all stopped and the workers were swarming towards the kilns. 'Where's the inspector? What happened to him? Was it the inspector?' he shouted as he ran. He felt a pang of guilt – the man had spoken to him just a couple of hours beforehand. What if the unfortunate victim had been the inspector? Alone on the Island, away from his family and friends? Kester began to run faster. It didn't take him long to reach the crowd of men. He pushed through them and they looked at the young man in their midst, identifying him as a stranger. Kester had an air about him that made the workers instinctively turn to him and trust him.

'It were Robbie, Sir. He just went in,' said one of the men. 'I saw him on the top. There were someone with him. And then he went. Sir, I'd say he was mebbe pushed...He just went all floppy, like. Then kind of folded up and went in. Then the flames started.'

'Who was with him?' asked Kester. 'Who witnessed it? Did the inspector see it? Where is he?' The noise from the kilns was deafening, the flames still shooting up into the sky as the man's body was incinerated within.

Kester looked around for his fellow passenger, but the man he was talking to shook his head. 'No inspectors here today, Sir. Nobody we were expecting. Don't know who it were up there with Robbie. Was that him, do you think? He was a stranger – didn't recognise him. Looked like he were dressed differently to us...' The worker gabbled on and Kester stared at him.

A sickening suspicion began in the pit of his stomach, and the horror crept up through his body. 'This man, this stranger you saw. Where is he now?'

'Dunno, Sir. What we going to do about Robbie, Sir? He'll be gone – no doubt about it.'

Kester shook his head helplessly. 'Your foreman? Could he help? Where is he? I will find him and speak to him.'

'He went around the back, Sir.' The man indicated the shore. Kester turned and ran along the track, towards the rolling waves of the North Sea.

'Please let me be in time,' he prayed as he ran, 'please let me save him.'

Kester rounded the corner and began to scramble through the sea grass and debris around the lime kilns. The shouts of the workers were still echoing around the area, mixed with the hissing and fizzing of the giant flames leaping out of the kiln. Quicklime was used for destroying infected bodies and slaked lime was used to disguise the reek of decaying flesh in mass burials. It had a power of its own – but Kester knew that something else on the Island that day was also dangerous and powerful. He ran, his heart pounding in his chest, until he saw the figure of the manager striding along in front of him.

He yelled at the man to stop. 'Hey! You, Sir! You are needed at the other side of the kilns!' he cried. 'There may have been another accident.' He thought quickly. 'A rogue spark – I believe it may have landed in the crowd. Your men, Sir, they need you!'

The foreman paused and turned around, his face white with shock. 'Pardon me?' he said. 'Another accident? But...'

'Just go. Go and see them,' gasped Kester, bending double as a stitch ripped into his side. 'Please,' he finished. He pointed vaguely in the direction he had just come from. 'You're needed....'

The foreman looked towards the sea. 'But there's a man – he might have seen something...'

'And he might not have done. I will find him,' said Kester, straightening up. 'I will deal with him.'

'If you're sure Sir,' said the foreman. He turned and began to hurry back to the crowds of workers. Kester sent a prayer of thanks up to God and prayed for forgiveness for lying to the man. It was for the greater good, though. He had probably just saved the foreman's life. Catching his breath again, he began to run towards the sea. He rounded a corner and the man who had travelled across the causeway with him appeared from behind a broken-down fisherman's shack. Kester stopped suddenly, inches from the man. Their eyes met, a mutual hatred registering between them.

'You should not have come here,' said the man. His face was still smeared with blood from the original kill – the man who had allegedly fallen into the lime kiln. 'You will be next. You know more than these folk do.' He bared his teeth in a snarl and Kester started as he saw the fangs. His courage must not fail him. His fingers closed around the hilt of the dagger.

'*You* should not have come here,' Kester replied. 'This is a holy place. There is no room for creatures such as yourself.'

24

'A holy place! Ha! I have travelled here from London town. I have killed in the very churchyard of St Paul's in Knightsbridge, just streets from my home. Holiness does not matter to me.'

'London?' said Kester, unable to stop himself. He remembered Summer, desperate to go to the family house in Grosvenor Square. *Life is more exciting there*, he remembered her saying, *I have friends there.*

The man laughed. 'I do not have to make conversation with you,' he said. 'You are worthless. I shall kill you, then kill the inhabitants of this pathetic little island one by one. The lime kilns can hide so much. The sea can wash away dead bodies. And maybe, if there is too much feasting to be had for myself alone, I shall summon my friends. Then, as I sit in my comfortable house replete, I might recall this little place fondly. I might even consider visiting another desolate, cut-off place. I hear the Scottish Isles are sparsely populated. I can spend quite some time there without drawing too much attention to myself.' He laughed. 'It is unfortunate, perhaps, that you have discovered me. Maybe I was rash. But I was hungry.' He shrugged his elegant shoulders. 'As I said, the time for conversation is over. It is time for you to die...' He lunged at Kester, who swiftly ripped the dagger out of his waistband.

Kester felt the breath of the vampire on his face and smelled the rusty odour of metallic, salty blood as it came near to him. But he was quick. He raised the dagger, just as the creature's hands grabbed his shoulders. Kester plunged the dagger into its body and threw himself to the side as the vampire screeched, disintegrating into dust only inches away from him.

'I'm not here for conversation,' Kester said. He stared at the ash on the ground. At least he had killed this one. And the other one in London. He knew he could do it. And he felt a trip to Knightsbridge was imminent.

***

Kester's family had a house in Grosvenor Square, in London. Situated in Mayfair, it was one of the most prestigious addresses in the Capital. The Lawson's owned a relatively small property in the Square, but it was still Grosvenor Square. Dukes, Duchesses and Members of Parliament were their neighbours. Summer had often been overwhelmed by the grandeur of the place. The carriages that rolled past the windows of the house transporting beautiful ladies and smart gentlemen had her in raptures. The houses seemed to swarm

25

with servants, and the Lawson's servants always seemed pleased to welcome the family, especially when they went to London for the Season. It still tugged at Kester's heart strings when he remembered how excited his sister had been about her coming-out ball. It was to be held in London, and there, it was assumed, she would meet a young man – hopefully titled – and live happily ever after. She had never experienced that. The sisters of their friends had fussed and preened and danced the Season away with scarcely a thought for Summer. Kester had been flirted with, cajoled and flattered, and had finally stopped attending the balls, much to his mother's despair. He had no interest in any of the girls. His sister should have been there. She had deserved to be there. He was just incidental.

Grosvenor Square, however, was not too far from St Paul's in Knightsbridge. It made Kester's skin crawl to think how close he might have been to that creature and his ilk every time he visited the City. Perhaps the vampire had seen Summer from the windows of a carriage? Perhaps the thing had even walked past their house in the Square, or lurked around the theatres, waiting for people to leave so it could follow them? It said it had killed in the churchyard. Kester, looking out of the window and staring at the Square's gardens, shuddered. The City could be seething with vampires: who would know? They walked amongst the people, looking and acting like humans, all the while searching for their next victim. Well, he had a lead, he supposed. He would start at the Square and wander through Knightsbridge. Sooner or later, he would come across something to help him; he had faith. One of the tall, graceful houses in that area held a secret, and he wasn't quite sure how he would discover which house it was. He looked about the airy, high-ceilinged room he stood in, and sipped the cup of tea a servant had brought him. People ventured in and out of these houses all day – ladies visiting other ladies, gentlemen calling in on business, nannies escorting numerous well-groomed, polished children... perhaps a vampire's house would be set apart by the *lack* of day to day activity? The vampire would probably live alone, surrounded by the wealth he had accrued over the decades. He might have servants; but perhaps they wouldn't act like normal ones. Would he have people calling on him? The vampire on Lindisfarne had mentioned that he had friends. What would his friends look like? Kester sighed. The words needle in a haystack sprang into his mind. There had to be something he could look out for. He might just have to walk the streets, watching the houses for a while. It was fortunate that the time of his visit did indeed coincide with the Season, so anything out of the ordinary in that respect would be worth looking out for, he reasoned. The Season generally lasted from April to August. It was now May. He had a little while yet before he outstayed his welcome in London.

***

The next day, Kester decided to begin his quest in earnest. He would start, he reasoned, with a walk through some of the most prestigious addresses of the capital, down towards Curzon Street, perhaps. The area around Curzon Street was a hub of wealth and beauty; things these vampires seemed to possess in great quantities. The roads around Grosvenor Square were busy, with carriages darting here and there and horses weaving between one another. Summer would have been in her element looking at the gowns the ladies wore, watching the people ride out towards Rotten Row in Hyde Park. Kester walked down South Audley Street and looked to his right. He could just see the Park through the streets, and once again felt the annoyance bubble up inside him. She had been just sixteen years old – a child. She should have been married now with several children. He walked faster, determined to find the house that this vampire had made his home. He walked up and down the side streets, back and forwards, staring at the houses; but nothing in any of them seemed out of character. Kester fought back a feeling of desperation. He couldn't give up now, that was inconceivable, but he really, truly, didn't know what else he could do. He rounded the corner and found himself on Curzon Street. He stopped. Where now? There wasn't exactly a convenient square or communal garden he could linger in. He would cross the road and walk slowly along the street, he decided, and see if anything unusual struck him. Failing that, he still had several miles of Mayfair and Knightsbridge to cover... all was not lost, he supposed.

The houses on Curzon Street were typical Mayfair residences; tall, elegant townhouses. He tried to look in the windows as he passed – one advantage of being on foot and the houses opening straight out onto the street. Through some of the windows he caught glimpses of family life. In one, a cat sat on the windowsill, until a small boy in an Eton collar pulled the animal away and hugged it to his cheek. In another, the front door opened to admit a young man twiddling his hat nervously between his hands; no doubt a suitor to a blushing young lady who was probably, at that very moment, having hysterics over what dress to wear to greet him. One house had

27

a maid in the window, dusting furiously. Her sharp little eyes darted to and fro along the street, maybe looking for her own suitor. And there he was, acknowledged Kester – an errand boy cycling furiously past. He slowed down as he passed the house, and took his hands off the handlebars, tucking them in his pockets, showing off to the maid as a smile broke across her pretty face and the boy winked at her in passing. So many lives, with so many little things happening: so many people unaware of the horror that resided in this city.

Kester continued ambling down Curzon Street, checking the houses as he went. His heart skipped a beat near the end of the road; one house in particular looked very interesting. It had dark drapes at the upstairs windows and the curtains at the front were almost closed. Kester paused and bent down as if he was fiddling with his boot fastening. He watched the house out of the corner of his eye and tried to catch a glimpse of the people who lived in it. Nothing seemed to be happening in the house. It appeared to be closed up and empty – highly unusual in this area during the Season. If a house wasn't owned by a family, it was rented out to one. Kester straightened up and looked at the house again. That was one to consider, he thought. He continued to the end of the street and nonchalantly turned around, ready to retrace his steps. He walked more slowly this time, his eyes on the closed up house with the apparently darkened rooms. A couple were walking towards him, the woman linking arms with the man. Neither was speaking and they seemed rather aloof. Kester's eyes narrowed. He slowed his steps even more and watched the couple turn and walk up to the front door of the shuttered house. The man rapped on the door smartly and they stood for a moment waiting for the door to open. Nothing happened. The couple looked at one another and the man rapped again. Still nothing. Not even a maid or a butler appeared to allow them access; even if the family were out, someone should have been in to answer the door, reasoned Kester. The couple stood for a moment more and the man leant down to the woman, whispering something in her ear. She nodded slightly and the man dropped what looked like a sealed envelope through the letterbox; then they turned around and stepped onto the pavement. They glided past Kester and he stood aside. A chill ran through his body as they passed him. The woman had lowered her head, but too late; Kester had already seen that her eyes were a deep shade of red.

The couple turned down the narrow lane of Derby Street. Beyond that, Kester knew, was the tiny street of Pitt's Head Mews. It was quiet down there. If anybody was walking along the Mews, it was unlikely there would be anyone around to hear their cries. Kester followed the couple, feeling the familiar jostle of the dagger against his hip. If he was wrong, he would only make himself look foolish. Rather that, than have this opportunity slip through his fingers.

'Excuse me!' he called. His voice sounded loud and out of place in the quiet lane. The couple stopped and the man turned around. The woman kept her face turned away from him. 'This may sound quite strange, but I couldn't help noticing that you were trying to visit a friend of mine a few moments ago.' Kester almost choked on the word 'friend'. How could that creature have been anyone's friend? 'I met him in Northumberland. He gave me that address, but I was unable to get an answer from the door. Do you know where he might be today?'

The man stared at Kester, seeming to weigh him up. 'You ask some strange questions, Sir,' he said. 'Why should I answer them?'

Kester felt the annoyance bubble up within him. Why were these things so bloody arrogant all the time? 'You do not have to answer me, Sir,' he replied. 'Certainly not. You do not have to explain yourself either. I was simply curious. I bid you farewell.' He nodded briefly and made as if he were to leave the alleyway. There was the faintest *whoosh* and he felt a cold breeze behind him. He turned, raising the dagger at the same moment the man reached out to grab him. The dagger found its mark; the vampire shrieked, exploding into a cloud of dust as it was slain. The vampire's partner screamed. She hurled herself at Kester, her eyes wild and blood-red. Kester struck once more and the blade landed between her breasts. She howled and stared at the dagger before collapsing into ash. It proved to Kester which house he needed to visit. Although, if he was honest with himself, he was unsure of what he hoped to find once he arrived there.

***

Tucking the dagger safely into his waistband, Kester pulled his waistcoat down to hide it, and shrugged his frock coat around him. Pushing his hands deep inside his pockets, he sauntered out of the alleyway back towards Curzon Street. All the while, he was planning the best way of entering the house. It seemed to him that his only option was through the back of it. He turned sharply onto Market Mews – the little street that would take him along the back of the terrace. He walked along to the end, assessing which house he needed to be at. There was a high brick wall along the back of the terrace, but there were gates leading out from each house on to the Mews. Kester was considering his chances of success, should he have to somehow break into a yard and clamber through the neighbouring ones until he got there, when he saw his opportunity. It was as if God was welcoming him; one of the gates was ajar. It was as if someone had left in a hurry and clashed the gate shut, but it hadn't caught on the latch and had bounced back. As he stood staring at it, Kester realised that this was, indeed, the house he had wanted to enter.

'Thank you, God,' he murmured, and pushed the door open wide enough for him to slip inside the yard. From the back, the house looked just as grim as the front did. He crouched down, keeping close to the dividing wall of the neighbouring house and made his way to the back door. He sensed that there was nobody around, but his heart still pounded in his chest. He felt around the door to see if that too was ajar, but it wasn't. Then he leaned his shoulder against it, to see if he could somehow open it with force. The door would not budge. He stood back and looked around him. He saw the basement window at ground level, and wondered if it was possible to drop down into the space and try to get in that way. He stood quietly, and pressed his ear against the back door, listening for sounds within the house. Nothing. He took a deep breath and stepped towards the basement space. In one movement, he was down in the gap. He hoped he could somehow get in – otherwise he was well and truly trapped.

The window slid upwards as many of them in these buildings did, and he tried to prise the pane up to gain access. A piece of rotten wood on the window sill suddenly gave way and it gave Kester's fingers enough purchase to push the pane up. The window moved – enough for him to slot both hands into the gap and continue to push it up with all his strength. The window creaked and groaned and sweat dripped down Kester's forehead. Eventually, it slid up and Kester was staring at a space wide enough for him to crawl through. This definitely led into the kitchens – and if a vampire lived here, he doubted that it would have need for a food preparation area such as this every day.

Kester slipped through the window and almost immediately his nostrils were assailed by a smell that made him gag. The whole room stank of rotting meat. He covered his mouth with his forearm and retched. He stumbled through the room and pushed open a door that he guessed led out into a corridor. The smell was worse here, if that were possible and he tripped over something on the floor.

'Dear God!' he cried, as he steadied himself. Lying on the floor was the decomposing remains of what he assumed had once been a scullery maid. He could just make out her white hat and apron in the gloom. He tried to push his way through another door, which at first resisted his efforts to open it. Partially blocking the door, at the bottom of a stone staircase, was what Kester assumed had once been a butler. He ran up the stairs and found himself in the main hallway of the house. Grand reception rooms led off from either side of it, the doors wide open. Through one door, Kester made out another body – a chamber maid, this time; still clutching a bunch of shrivelled flowers in her hand. A footman, dressed in golden livery was huddled by the front door. Thick masses of flies buzzed around the place and Kester ran up another flight of stairs. Door after door stood open; a similar scene greeting him in many of the rooms. He did not dare investigate the dining room too thoroughly; one glance was enough to satisfy him that the bodies of several people, men and women, were ranged around a table covered with blood and broken crockery. The body of a young girl was amongst them; her eyes stared sightlessly out of the door towards Kester and she reminded him somehow of his sister. He made the sign of the cross and closed the door to the room, feeling utterly helpless. It was as if something had purged the house of all life; and Kester decided that this carnage could not possibly be the result of one creature's greed. It was more than likely the work of the vampire he had met on Lindisfarne, assisted by his elegant, hungry friends.

Kester made his way through some more rooms. One small room which led off a hallway was devoid of bodies and seemed to be a study or a library of some description. He moved over to the walnut desk which sat in the middle of the room and pulled the drawers out. He rifled through the contents of the drawers one by one: household bills and accounts, advertisements, old scribbled notes – the usual detritus of day to day life. He wanted to find something which would give him a clue as to where the vampire's friends resided. The vampires he had encountered were well-dressed, cultured looking individuals. They could be swarming around Mayfair and Kensington for all he knew. He was willing to bet that the one who had killed his sister was from the area. For a fleeting moment, he wondered if the vampires actually bred – whether the couple he had seen today, perhaps, had any children? He doubted it. Reason and research told him vampires only increased the number of their species by choosing victims which they changed. The thought was abhorrent to him – not just the changing, but the thought of them making love and acting like animals. Surely there could be nothing loving about it? Did they even have feelings?

The smell of gore and decay was getting stronger in the warm afternoon as the house heated up and the sun filtered through the shutters at the back. He had to work quickly before he vomited. He didn't think he would be disturbed; on some level, he trusted that the man on Lindisfarne had been the hub of the activity in this house and that man was, of course, no longer a danger. Kester wondered why he had killed his servants though, as well as the dinner guests. Had they seen too much, or had his friends become greedy? Or were the guests, indeed, the main course? He didn't want to think about it too deeply. He felt around in the desk and pulled more bits of paper out; nothing. He stared around the study, thwarted; then he remembered the couple pushing something through the letterbox, moments before he had confronted them.

'That's it!' Kester cried. His voice echoed around the house, breaking the incessant buzzing of the bluebottles. The letterbox; his stomach churned at the thought of going too near the body of the footman, but he had no choice.

Kester made his way down the stairs, the bile rising in his throat with every step. He saw the footman propped up by the door and pulled a face, trying not to inhale as he leant down to pick up the letter. Inches away from the bloodied corpse, he caught sight of a movement out of the corner of his eye. He yelled as the footman's hand suddenly reached out, the fingers curling tightly around his wrist.

The footman laughed and began to stand up, almost pulling Kester to the floor. Kester's foot slipped in a pool of blood; he knew that if he fell now, he would have no chance at all. The footman, or whatever he was, would be at an advantage.

'Too late for 'em,' rasped the vampire. 'They got 'em. They got 'em all except me. I disturbed 'em, you see, but they didn't finish

me off. They'd been too well fed. Not much feeding left here now.'
The vampire shook Kester like a puppet, dangling him a few inches up in the air, then dropping him down and so he skidded around on the bloody floor.

'They were disturbed before they could finish me off, you see. I've been eatin' up their leftovers, just waitin' here on my own; but fresh blood is better. You'll do for fresh blood. I've finished with them gentlefolks now.'

Kester writhed, held fast by his wrist. Swearing and shouting, he struggled against the clearly insane footman, who was now laughing at him in delight. 'You're lively, nice and lively,' the footman was saying. 'You'll make a good meal, you will.' Kester twisted once more and managed to reach across his torso. He grabbed the dagger with his left hand and wasted no time in plunging it into the footman's body. The vampire looked startled and the pressure on Kester's wrist disappeared as the creature evaporated into dust. Kester, breathing heavily, stared at the heap of ash. His idea of a clever, elegant person was challenged. An apparently newborn vampire left to fend for itself, seemingly had no more social skills than the next person. This problem was possibly more widespread than he had ever imagined.

Kester listened to the silence of the house which was overlaid with the beating of his heart and the repulsive buzzing of the flies. He prayed that no more vampires would appear in that beautiful, yet evil, residence. He tried to calm himself, telling himself that there was nothing there now except human death. He must focus on his task and for that, he would need the letter. Stepping across the remains of the footman, he picked up the envelope, opened it and began to read the gracefully formed script. The author had been astute. There was no address and no name: but, reading between the lines, Kester formed his own opinion of what the letter suggested;

"I thank you for inviting us to your recent house party. It seems a fair length of time since we enjoyed such a substantial meal. One does forget that one needs to curb one's appetite at times; and it is a pity that the guests and particularly the staff were not more compliant. Disturbances never suit me, but I suspect we will not be bothered again. I regret any unfinished business, and offer my sincere apologies; but we must live for the future and I believe we may now have found the ideal area for our next 'dinner'. New Gravel Lane is the perfect place – too many suicides from the bridge have occurred in recent months to cause any concern. We hope to have the pleasure of your company very soon. The area

may not be quite to your taste, used as you are, to a more refined environment, but it serves us very well. Once again, thank you for your hospitality. The pleasure was immeasurable. I trust I shall be seeing you upon your return from the North. Best regards."

Kester stared at the letter. New Gravel Lane. An area as far removed from Mayfair as it was possible to be. New Gravel Lane was near the docks – part of the East End and a notorious suicide spot as the author suggested. The perfect place, in fact, for people to disappear with no questions asked. Kester looked around the hallway, thinking. He re-read the letter and made his decision. There was obviously a group of these creatures in the East End; somewhere near the Ratcliffe Highway. Fifty years ago, there had been some high profile murders in the area – nobody had been formally convicted. People still talked about the killings and he had learned something about them over the years, especially from some of the older servants at Grosvenor Square. Nobody was ever formally convicted, but the main suspect had hanged himself and been buried with a stake through his heart at a crossroads. Exactly how vampires were buried. Kester did not think for one moment that the accused had been a vampire – vampires did not die by simply hanging themselves. But for the locals to bury him as they had done...was it purely coincidence? He shuddered.

Fired up by the new information, Kester determined to take himself to the East End and establish where these creatures were living; if possible, he would kill every last one of them. He made his way slowly out of the hallway and walked towards the back of the house. He was fairly sure that the owner was never coming back and there was now nobody around to let anybody else in. He would leave by the back door, head out through the Mews onto the main road and hail a cab. It was the quickest way to the docks, New Gravel Road and the Ratcliffe Highway.

***

The Ratcliffe Highway was deep within the slums of the East End, running for a mile through London. It was the haunt of villains, murderers and prostitutes. Amongst the Rookeries, shadowy figures slipped about their business. Nobody questioned them. Nobody dared enter the area, unless they had no choice. Kester had a choice. He knew what to expect and he knew what he might find there. He felt the hilt of the dagger close to his body and sent a prayer up to the Lord above.

34

'Lookin' for somethin', Sir?' came a voice. Kester jumped and turned. A young girl, sixteen, seventeen maybe, slunk out of the filthy gloom of an alleyway and tilted her head to one side. She smiled up at Kester, her hand on her hip. 'I can probably help, Sir,' she continued, 'if you let me, Sir. If you pay me right, Sir.'

'No. No, there is nothing you can help me with, thank you.' he replied and turned away from her. He didn't like conversation at the best of times.

'Go on, Sir. I can, you know. Don't see your type 'round here much. You got to be lost or lookin' for somethin', aincha? Don't lie to me.' She smiled again and sidled up to him. Kester shrank away from her, almost automatically. The girl was as filthy as the alley she had come from. Dirt ingrained her face and her sludge coloured hair was pulled into a rough topknot. A ribbon which possibly used to be a bright scarlet, was wound around her head and the ends of the ribbon hung lank and frayed down the side of her face.

Kester's eyes dropped down and saw that she was obviously pregnant. 'Good Lord,' he whispered.

The girl followed his gaze and laughed. She rubbed her belly. 'Turns some men on, that does,' she said. 'Not you then?'

'Please – just go. Go and take care of yourself,' he said.

'Nah, can't go back yet Sir,' she said. 'It ain't right. Not 'til I made some money for him at any rate.' She pressed her hand into the small of her back. 'You sure Sir? I'll make it worth your while.'

'For God's sake...here. Take this and go away,' said Kester, pulling his leather wallet out from beneath his coat. He longed for the girl to disappear back into the alleyways and giving her money seemed to be the quickest way to chase her. He rifled around for some coins. 'Tell whoever you answer to that you made it...doing whatever you do.'

The girl laughed softly. 'You're a good 'un, Sir,' she said. The coins disappeared somewhere inside her shawl. 'What's that you got?' she asked, nodding towards Kester's waist. 'Seems awful nice to be carrying here. Protection is it? You oughter be careful, Sir.'

'Thank you. I am quite capable of looking after myself,' muttered Kester. His eyes travelled around the alleyways, taking in the closely packed houses. He suspected this was the right place, he could feel it. This was the very place they would come to. They could lose themselves here and nobody would ever know where they were.

Nobody would come into this area without a jolly good reason. The bridge wasn't far away so that would be a good place to start...

'You gotta be extra careful around here, Sir,' said the young girl.

'Please, can't you just leave me alone?' snapped Kester, turning his back on her.

'You don't realise, Sir. Anything could happen,' she replied.

And Kester didn't know what had hit him. The girl leapt at him, knocking him off his feet. He tried to struggle up, scrabbling in vain for the dagger, but the girl was strong. She pinned him down and bent over him. 'Anything could happen,' she hissed. She bared her teeth and brought her face down to his neck.

Kester's screams were ignored as his life was taken from him. Just more screams in the Rookeries from another fool who had strayed too close to Ratcliffe Highway. The girl stood up, and smiled, blood dripping from her mouth. She wiped her face on the back of her hand, and bent over Kester's body, stripping him of his wallet. She pulled his cloak to one side and ripped the silver dagger from his waistband. She looked around and slipped back into the alleyway. She lifted her shawl and pulled out the bundle of rags she had stuffed her own clothes with. She replaced them with the dagger and, looking around once more, melted away into the Rookeries.

She had no idea what the dagger was for. There'd been a few stories recently, granted. But that's all they were at the end of the day: stories. Be something to keep such a pretty thing, though: it was nice and shiny and might even be worth a few bob, she thought.

Present Day

Guy looked up from his notes as he heard the shouts and clattering of visitors, feet and luggage coming along the corridor - the history students, he realised. Christine, the landlady, had told him last night she was expecting a crowd of young lads. She was fussing at the fact she might not be able to keep them fed. She had the place filled for three days at least, and he had three days to concentrate on his research whilst she was otherwise engaged.

There was a final slam of the door, a few minutes after everyone else had been shepherded to their rooms by Christine. Guy caught sight of a tall, sandy haired lad hovering in the corridor, looking around, apparently hoping that someone would appear to show him to his room.

'Lucas!' hollered a voice from the highest landing. 'Up here, mate. We got the attic room. That's OK isn't it? Come and pick your bed. There's one left.' Guy heard a guffaw of laughter. 'Sorry, mate, couldn't resist. Good view of the pub from the window. Good to keep an eye on the locals.' The boy laughed again. His voice faded slightly. 'Come on, hurry up. We've got work to do.'

Guy got up and moved to the door, pushing it open slightly. The lad he assumed was Lucas, was climbing the stairs two at a time. Guy had a strange feeling about this one. He worked on instinct most of the time, and he was picking up something here; something that just didn't feel right. He watched Lucas until he disappeared, then closed the door softly. He went back to the table he was working at and took a sip of cold coffee, pulling a face as he did so. He brought the morning newspaper closer to him and read the article for the hundredth time.

Genevieve de Havilland stared up at the frost, which glimmered against the wall of the ruined chapel. Half covered in lichen and moss, the arch, which once held a stained glass window, looked blindly out across the white countryside. An abandoned nest hung from the weather-worn bricks in the corner, and Genevieve put one gloved hand up to it. The decaying twigs crumbled under her touch, and she rubbed her finger-tips together, breaking up the dusty greyness. She turned to Will Hartley, fixing him with dark eyes. The young man was leaning against a gravestone, his black hair stark against the whiteness of the moors and the grey stonework of the chapel.

'So is this the last time we'll be together?' Genevieve asked. 'When do you have to leave?'

'Tomorrow morning,' he said.

'And when will you be back?'

'I don't know. My father is entertaining colleagues from Europe tonight. I'm supposed to travel with them tomorrow but nobody has mentioned coming back.'

'And what are they trying to achieve by doing this?'

'I do believe they are trying to keep us apart,' he said. He pushed himself away from the stone and held his hand out to her. 'You are asking a lot of questions.'

'You told me you would marry me,' she said, ignoring the gesture. 'Come tonight, Will. Come to the Hall instead. We will tell them there and then.' She smiled to herself. 'Now wouldn't that upset my mother's plans?'

'I would love nothing better, but I have to abide by my father's wishes.'

'No, you don't,' she said. She stared at him, waiting for him to reply, but he simply smiled and held his hand out again.

'It's not that easy. We may need to wait a little longer than we intended.'

Genevieve scowled. She took Will's hand and he led her to her horse, a white mare which was pulling at some frozen stalks of grass.

'You won't stay away long,' she stated. 'Do you understand?'

'I understand,' said Will.

'I don't want you away from me,' said Genevieve. 'You are to come tonight and I will see you then.' She mounted the horse and whipped it, cantering off without waiting for an answer. She wondered briefly whether Will would rather risk her displeasure, or his family's. She would make things very difficult for him if he chose his family tonight over her.

***

Genevieve cantered through the wintery moorland, the sun glinting off the white branches and dazzling her eyes. She was eighteen now and had apparently been 'marriageable' for a year or so. Her mother and brother were planning a ball for her that night; in Genevieve's opinion, it was a calculated, deliberate way to separate her from Will. She slowed Star to a trot as she approached the front of the Hall, the pathway swept through the gardens where oddly shaped lumps and bumps in the snowdrifts signified plants and shrubs. Someone had made an effort to clear the steps up to the house, and Genevieve saw a few of the manservants digging a channel away from the house down the drive. She continued towards the house, weaving Star around the sweep of the drive and bringing the horse to a halt by the mounting block at the side. A servant ran across to her and helped her down. She picked her way towards the steps, holding her skirts up out of the way. The day was already darkening and Genevieve hurried up the steps into the hallway. The lamps had been lit inside and a fire was crackling in the grate. A maid appeared and curtsied to her, taking her gloves and hat, and Genevieve started to climb the stairs to the first floor. She could hear her mother complaining about something in the library.

'I am just as pleased that man is going away. It's the best thing. He should have been sent away sooner. I blame them both.'

Genevieve's heart skipped a beat and she stopped on the stairs. She leant across the banister, listening as Lady de Havilland ranted on. She gripped the banister tightly, the anger bubbling up inside of her. This was ridiculous. They weren't the ones who had committed a crime. She leaned further over the banister and took a deep breath.

'Does it matter?' she shrieked. 'Does it really matter? He will marry me and I'm not open to any other suggestions.'

Her mother's voice juddered into shocked silence. The door of the library banged open and her brother stormed out. 'That's enough!' Joseph snapped.

Genevieve headed back down the staircase and faced him. Five years older than her, she had never liked him.

'Enough?' she cried. 'I will not be attending the ball and I do not have to prove anything.' She turned and pushed past Joseph into the study, slamming the door behind her.

Joseph caught it and threw it open again, storming in after her. 'It's the least you can do,' he hissed. 'It's only a ball. If Hartley was coming, you would be there.'

Genevieve narrowed her eyes. 'Oh dear, did you forget to invite him. Don't worry, I've asked him and he's coming.'

Joseph lowered his voice dangerously. 'It's time you left the Hall. Nobody wants you here, but we have to be seen to do it properly.'

'I'm so sorry that I destroyed your plans, dear brother,' replied Genevieve, equally dangerously. 'I could have been gone by now, but I ruined it, didn't I? What a shame.'

Joseph raised his hand, his eyes blazing. 'How dare you...' he started.

Genevieve moved quickly out of his way and grabbed a lethal-looking paper-knife from a desk. 'Violence solves everything, doesn't it?' she said. 'Will would never even raise his *voice* to me.'

Joseph dropped his hand. 'You try my patience,' he growled.

'As you try mine,' she replied. She still held the knife out in front of her. *One day...one day...*

'You would do well to consider other people,' shouted Joseph. 'There is no future for you and Hartley: accept it.' He turned and slammed his way out of the study, punching the side of a bookcase as he left.

'Will and I are destined be together!' Genevieve yelled after him. '*You* should accept *that.*'

She suddenly realised that she was still holding the knife. She looked at it with some incomprehension for a moment, then laid it down carefully, exactly in the centre of the desk.

***

There was no way to get out of it. At seven o'clock, Genevieve was standing at the top of the grand staircase, looking down into the hall. Everything was decorated in blues and silver and tiny candles flickered and sparkled, reflected in the hallway mirrors.

40

Lady de Havilland had ensured Genevieve's gown co-ordinated perfectly with the theme. The dress was white and ice blue, and had tiny pearls sewn on here and there with silver thread. The skirt swept back to a full bustle at the back, and the train spread softly out on the staircase. Genevieve wore a blue and silver ribbon around her throat and her dark hair had been brushed until it shone. It was swept up on the top of her head, with one long ringlet falling forward across her shoulder. Lady de Havilland had also sent a maid to remind Genevieve that she needed to make a good impression. This had rankled with Genevieve. Why would she want to do that? She was going to marry Will Hartley. Genevieve made her way carefully down the stairs, her white satin slippers peeping out from beneath her skirts. She judged the distance to the door, wondering if she could walk straight out into the night, but there was to be no such luck. Joseph appeared from the flickering shadows. He silently offered her his arm and she stared at him. It repulsed her to even think about touching him.

'Ready?' he asked, without smiling.

'Why are you waiting here?' she countered.

'To ensure you attend,' he replied.

'I have other plans,' she said and made to walk past him.

Joseph caught her by the wrist and she winced as his fingers tightened around it. He was a strong man and held her fast. 'You will come with me,' he said and steered her towards the doorway.

Genevieve tried to pull away from him, but he twisted her wrist, squeezing his fingers against the white skin. She felt the bones crush slightly and gasped. Joseph pushed her towards the ballroom, and a footman threw open the door and bowed to Genevieve as she was forced past him. Genevieve knew that the staff would not get involved with the family disputes. One sleight, implied or explicit, and Joseph would ensure they were dismissed.

The orchestra began to play a grand, triumphal, processional piece and Genevieve's cheeks burned as the guests all turned to watch her enter. She cast a glance around the room, trusting that Will had arrived and defied everyone, but he wasn't there. A venomous look flashed briefly across her face as her mother appeared by her shoulder.

'I have worked extremely hard for this,' said Lady de Havilland. 'Don't you *dare* let me down.'

'Is Will Hartley here yet?' Genevieve asked. 'He is coming, you know.'

'That man is not welcome at the Hall!' hissed her mother.

'He's coming. I invited him... ouch!' Joseph dug his nails into Genevieve's arm and she clamped her lips together. She had made her point.

A young man peeled away from the crowds and walked towards them. Lady de Havilland noticed, and turned to Joseph, snatching the opportunity to divert the conversation.

'Joseph dear,' she said, raising her voice and smiling at the stranger. 'Please would you do us the honour?'

'Montgomery?' said Joseph. He looked confused.

'The very same,' smiled the man. 'So good of you to invite me.' Joseph frowned slightly and the young man laughed. 'Oh, it wasn't you then? Well. I have one of you to thank for the invitation at any rate.' He smiled again, a lazy, confident smile. The man took Genevieve's hand and bowed over it politely.

Joseph looked at him for a moment. 'Oh. Of course. Well, since you are here, let me introduce you to my sister, Miss Genevieve de Havilland,' he said. 'You may as well meet her. The ball is supposed to be for her, although she isn't exactly grateful for it.'

Genevieve glared at her brother and forced herself to look down at Montgomery's fair head as he stood up to face her.

'I am absolutely charmed to meet you, Miss de HavillandH,' he said.

He smiled into her eyes and Genevieve stared back at him thoughtfully. 'My brother has mentioned you in the past,' she said finally. 'Didn't you go to Oxford together? Dear Joseph did tell us that your estate had run into terrible difficulties last year and you had come to him for advice. I understand that he didn't want to become involved, he said you had a lot of work to do before you could make it viable. I find it hard to believe you have achieved all that within a few short months. I also find it hard to believe that my brother has welcomed you back under such circumstances.'

Montgomery laughed easily and looked around at the shocked faces of Genevieve's family. Joseph's face had darkened and Genevieve knew his fists would be clenched, the skin of his knuckles straining white across the bone. She would pay for her insolence later, she guessed.

'My lady?' asked Montgomery and offered her his arm. 'I would be enchanted to look after you for a little while. If your family will excuse us?'

'She is excused,' said Joseph. He glared at Genevieve. 'I will, of course, come and find you later on.' Genevieve was aware of the thinly veiled threat the words held. Well, she would be ready for him this time.

Montgomery nodded to the de Havillands and guided Genevieve away from them, out onto the dance floor. He took her hand in his and held her gently around the waist. He looked down at her and smiled again. 'Yes, what you said before was quite correct, Miss de Havilland. Your brother made me understand my limitations and I had to make some difficult choices.'

'One of my brother's strengths is to make one understand one's limitations. Should one not understand them, he will educate one until one does understand them. I tend not to spend too much time with my family if I can help it,' Genevieve said. 'I dislike their education.'

'Is there anybody you would rather spend your time with, Miss de Havilland?' said Montgomery. Genevieve glared at him and a quizzical expression passed across his face. 'I see,' he said. 'Or perhaps I don't see. Tell me, is he here tonight?'

'As you say, Sir, sometimes we have to make difficult choices,' answered Genevieve. 'He apparently chose not to come tonight. If he was here, I would be spending my time with him rather than you.'

'Ah, I feel that there is more to this story than meets the eye. Perhaps one day I shall find out why he isn't here.'

'Perhaps. Oh dear, that's the music ending, how dreadful,' she said as the final notes died away. 'A round of applause for our musicians?' She managed to release herself from his hold and turned to face the orchestra. She clapped politely, aware of her partner doing the same behind her.

'I enjoyed that, Miss de Havilland,' he said. 'May I mark your card for another dance?' Without waiting for an answer, he plucked the card that was tied at her wrist and studied it. He carefully pencilled his name next to a dance further down the list. Genevieve hated such formalities. Will would have just asked her outright. 'Veva,' he might have said, 'would you?' He was the only one who

43

ever called her Veva. She would never allow anybody else to use that name.

'Would you please excuse me?' Genevieve said to Montgomery. 'I shall no doubt see you later.' In that moment, she swore to herself that she would go over to Hartside and drag Will out of his business meeting if he didn't turn up. What did she care for propriety after all? Her brother rammed that trait down her throat constantly. She might as well prove him right. Montgomery half smiled. He bowed and stepped aside. Genevieve headed off across the dance floor, towards the French doors. The ballroom was stuffy and oppressive and she slipped behind the heavy curtains, easing the doors open. They led onto some steps which ran down into the garden, and the yellow light from the ballroom spilled out onto the white landscape before her. Keeping close to the house, she edged her way around the building until she reached the servants' entrance and peeped inside. There was laughter and chattering coming from the kitchen and from the room with the scrubbed wooden table where the staff congregated for meals. Genevieve padded quietly in and reached out to a peg which hung behind the door. She unhooked a heavy, velvet cloak and wrapped it around herself. She took a deep breath of the frosty night air and, draping the train of her skirt over her arm, she began to hurry down the pathway into the walled garden. She lost her footing once or twice on the icy pathways, and headed towards the summer house. Reaching the summer house, she pushed the door open and waited a moment until her eyes adjusted.

The white, moonlit night filtered in through the leaded windows and highlighted a wrought iron picnic set, left in the summer house over the winter. An old chaise longue was there as well, the material frayed slightly at the sides and on the cushions. Genevieve knelt down by the fireplace and poked around until she found enough fuel to light the fire, then sat down on the chaise longue, folding herself inside the cloak and watching the flames lick the chimney. She would stay here as long as possible. And maybe go straight to Hartside afterwards. She sat back and imagined Will's face if she turned up uninvited and demanded he left with her in front of the businessmen. Her mouth twisted slightly into a little smile. It would be cruel, but no less than he deserved. She became aware of the pencil from her dance card jangling against her wrist and she ripped the card off in disgust. She studied her wrist in the firelight. The bruises were starting to come through. The idiot; he hadn't been as careful as usual. People might see those ones. He hadn't thought it out. Perversely pleased that she had unintentionally scored a point against her brother, she smiled to herself. She briefly contemplated damaging her wrist a little more, just to make sure people noticed. She was on the verge of doing so, when a shadow passed the window of the summerhouse. It blotted out the moonlight for a moment and she looked up, assuming it was tree branches. She sighed. Bored of her wrist, or perhaps simply forgetting her intentions, she went back to contemplating the fire. She began to hum a little tune, slightly off-key, and pulled her cloak tighter around her body. She leaned forward to poke at the embers of the fire and the flames whooshed up again. The wood crackled, spitting sparks out and singeing her dress. She tutted and tried to brush the marks off. Then there was another noise – the noise of the door handle being tried, and then a scraping sound as the door began to open.

Genevieve grabbed the poker and watched the door. It creaked fully open and a figure stood in the doorway. The figure was dressed from head to foot in black; it appeared to be a man, swathed in a cape with a hat pulled down low over his brow. Genevieve's grasp tightened.

'Joseph!' she said. 'I swear to God, I will kill you if you touch me...'

The man laughed. 'I'm not going to hurt you. Put the poker down, Veva.' He stepped into the summer house, the light from the fire picking out gold flecks in his dark eyes.

'Will!' Genevieve threw the poker down and it clattered onto the floor. She stood up. 'What are you doing here? Why not be a man and come to the house? Are you scared of my brother?' she laughed cynically. 'Yes, I suppose you could be. It's understandable, I suppose. How did you know I'd be here?'

'So many questions,' said Will. 'Again. Why do you ask so many? But tonight the answer is simple. I wanted to see you, so I came. For your information, I did come to the house; I was hiding in the trees across the lawn. I saw you dancing.' He frowned. 'Who was it?'

'A friend of my brother's,' replied Genevieve. Will said nothing, waiting for her to elaborate. She held his gaze. 'He's nobody important, don't worry. Why didn't you come inside, Will?'

'I took a chance coming over here tonight anyway,' said Will, taking the hat off and laying it on the table next to Genevieve's discarded dance card. He picked up the card. 'Oh, I say, Montgomery has a title. How nice. Anyway, darling, I might be mistaken,' he said, 'but wouldn't you rather be in the house, enjoying the ball, than being out here in the cold?' He The man nodded his head towards the house. 'It seems as if they have a new dance starting. I can hear the music.'

Genevieve said nothing. She looked over Will's shoulder in the direction of the house then spoke. 'No. I think I'd rather be here actually.' She looked at him again and a slow smile spread across her lips. 'Having considered it, I quite like you in that outfit, Will Hartley.' The meaning in her words was obvious. 'But tell me, how did you escape from that business dinner?'

'Quite easily,' he said, 'but let's not talk about where I should be. Let's talk about you. In fact, I've made a decision. I don't think you should go back yet either.' He took her hand and raised it up to his lips. 'If I should delay you here, who else will be disappointed tonight? Apart from our friend Montgomery?'

'Nobody,' said Genevieve. She felt her cheeks grow warm as Will studied her face. She tried to control her breathing as he stood up, still holding her hand.

'I don't think I particularly like Montgomery,' he said. 'Why should he have you tonight?' He leaned closer to her ear and whispered, 'I wouldn't want you to rush off to be with him.' Will stood upright and used his free hand to scoop her hair away from the side of her face. She reached up and covered his hand with hers, looking straight into his eyes. He traced the line of her face with his fingers and dropped his hand from the side of her face. He cupped her chin. Genevieve caught her breath. 'Ahhh, but not yet,' he said. 'It's wrong for you to miss out on the dancing.' He bowed low and held his hand out to her. 'Will you dance with me tonight?'

He took hold of Genevieve around the waist and pulled her close to him. The material of his cloak was scratchy against her face and he smelled of frost and ice and outdoors. Genevieve did not resist. She closed her eyes and began moving with him to the faint music that spilled out from the Hall. When the music fell silent, Will pulled her closer to him. Genevieve found his lips on hers and, almost instinctively, she closed her eyes and gave herself up to him.

***

46

Afterwards, they lay on the chaise longue, covered by the cloaks. The fire had burned down to the embers, all warmth dissipating with the flames. Genevieve sat up in the freezing room and pulled the cloak closer to her.

'Are you still going away tomorrow?' she asked Will. 'Are you still leaving me?'

'It won't be too long before I'm back,' he said. He touched his hand to her face. 'But I didn't want to leave without seeing you tonight.'

'So you're doing what they want.' she stated.

Will didn't reply. Instead, he sat up and fumbled for his shirt. 'I don't have a choice,' he said.

'Yes, you do.'

'No. I can't take the chance of Joseph finding out about us again. If I stay, he could make things even more difficult for you.'

'I can look after myself,' protested Genevieve. 'I can make things difficult for him. And for you.'

'Joseph is dangerous, Veva,' said Will, 'we both know that.' Genevieve unconsciously looked down at her wrist and rubbed it. Will followed her glance. 'What was that for?'

'I didn't want to go to the ball,' she replied. 'It's nothing.'

Will picked up her hand and kissed her wrist. 'I wish I could take you with me,' he said.

'You could if you wanted to,' she replied, watching him get dressed.

'Maybe another time. Let me get this trip out of the way first,' he said. 'So, until we meet again,' he touched her face one last time and dropped a kiss on her cheek, 'goodbye, Veva.' He turned away, slipping through the door and disappearing into the gardens. Genevieve remained under the cloak, watching the door shut. She reached around to the back of her head and unclasped a diamond-encrusted comb. She swept her hair back from her face trying to tidy it up and fixed the comb back in. She pulled her gown towards her and, shivering, she eased herself back into it, never taking her eyes off the door. Was that it then? Had he really gone? She felt numb. She hadn't felt like that last time. Last time, he had told her that he loved her.

***

Genevieve damped down what was left of the fire and the ashes smouldered in the grate. She left the summer house, closing the door behind her. She gathered the cloak around her and wound her way back through the gardens towards the Hall. Her satin slippers were ruined, soaking wet and covered in grey slush. She couldn't feel her toes. The door to the servants' quarters was as she had left it and she took off the cloak and threw it back in the room. Someone was bound to find it and hang it up. She retraced her steps around the side of the house and tried to smooth her hair back, then she straightened her shoulders and pushed the French doors open. She squeezed through the gap and stepped back into the ballroom, feeling the colour flood her cheeks with the warmth of the room. Genevieve looked around at the hustle and bustle, so different from the peace and quiet in the summer house. Guests were talking and laughing, pushing through the various knots of people to reach the refreshments table or to sit on a chair at the side of the room. The smell of so many candles mingled with the ladies' perfume made her feel sick.

'Where have you been?' asked Joseph, appearing beside her. The man missed nothing. His eyes raked over her, searching, it seemed, for some evidence of a misdemeanour.

'I needed some air,' Genevieve said.

'Air?' said Joseph. 'Don't lie to me. Where is he? What were you doing with him? Or need I ask?'

'So many questions,' replied Genevieve, almost mechanically. She looked around the ballroom and spotted Montgomery, standing alone. He turned to see her watching him and smiled, raising a glass to her. Joseph took a step towards her, his face twisted in disgust. Over his shoulder, Genevieve saw Montgomery place his glass on a table began to walk across to them.

'Excuse me, dear brother,' Genevieve said. 'I believe this dance is marked on my card. I would hate to disappoint your friend.' She moved away from Joseph, and began to walk towards Montgomery. She had understood that look on Joseph's face all too well.

'Miss de Havilland.' Sir Montgomery bowed as she approached him. 'Is it time for our dance? I do hope so.' He took her hand and lifted it to see the dance card. Too late, she realised she had left the card in the summer house. And too late, he had seen the circlet of darkening bruises around her wrist. He lifted his eyes to meet hers and she tried to snatch her hand away. Montgomery held onto it, his eyes burning into hers. Genevieve stole a glance at her brother who was watching them, his face thunderous. The corners of her lips twitched into a harsh little smile. So, somebody here had noticed as well. Her half-smile was enough for Montgomery to realise what had happened and he let her hand drop.

'I see,' he said. 'It's very noisy, isn't it? I could do with a change of scenery and some peace and quiet. Where do you recommend?'

'Anywhere but here,' replied Genevieve.

Montgomery bowed slightly and offered his arm. 'Then shall we leave?' he asked.

***

Genevieve tolerated him until they reached the library. Then she threw his hand off her and began to pace around the room.

'I hate being touched,' she muttered. 'It's like him doing it all over again. So, you can go now.'

She was aware of Montgomery moving over to the fireplace and watching her. She didn't care. She was remembering Will, realising suddenly that he had left her with barely a backwards glance. If she allowed herself to process the thought thoroughly, she would feel cheapened. Instead, it was nice to recall, with perfect clarity how his hand had felt on her waist and how her skin had tingled as all the nerve endings leapt into life...

'You don't make things easy for me, Miss de Havilland,' Montgomery said, interrupting her tangled thoughts. Genevieve's head snapped around and she stared at him. She focussed on him, wondering for half a second what he was doing with her in the summer house. Then her mind cleared. 'In what way?' she asked.

'I'm just intrigued. Is there something you wish to tell me? Maybe I can help.'

Genevieve brightened. 'Could you perhaps, erase my family from my life?' She laughed. 'Yes. Actually, I think that might solve all my problems.' She looked down at her wrist and moved over to Montgomery. She lifted her hand up to his eye-level. 'You saw this. You know what happens here,' she said. 'But this is nothing. Believe me.' She began to pull out her hair combs and clips one by one, letting her hair fall in a dark curtain down over her shoulders. She had no intention of going back into that ballroom tonight. 'Make my apologies for me. Tell them I have a headache,' she said.

'If that is what you wish,' said Montgomery. 'May I?' he came closer to her and raised his hand. She flinched. 'I'm sorry – I just want to help,' he said. 'I'm not your brother.' She felt a pull as a clip was taken out of the back of her hair. Montgomery bowed and presented her with it.

She paused for a moment, then took it from him. 'I apologise,' she said. 'Joseph is normally much more discreet.'

'It's not your fault,' Montgomery said.

'Thank you,' said Genevieve, gathering her combs together and flinging them into the fire, 'but it is. You see, it's all my fault. Joseph keeps telling me that.' She turned and glided out of the library, the soft rustle of her dress soothing against the cracking and spitting of the flames in the old fireplace. Halfway up the stairs, her mind went blank. She paused and smoothed her dress down, wondering why it had such burn holes in it. Not to worry. It wasn't as if she was wearing it for a special occasion.

**

Once she had reached the top of the stairs, Genevieve hurried along the corridor towards her room. She pushed the door open and it slammed shut behind her. She pressed her weight against it, locking it securely with the big iron key. She left the key in the lock. She'd already learned to do that. Not stopping to remove her dress, she threw herself onto the bed. She thought again about Will and the fact that he was leaving her. What if that evening in the summer house had actually been their last? What if she waited for him and he never came back at all?

Someone began hammering on her door and shouting through the keyhole. She pulled a pillow over her head and muffled everything out. She knew that eventually she would fall asleep. She always did.

Genevieve woke up with a start, the shouting and noise staying with her. She was still lying on the top of her bed, in her ballgown, although the dress was crumpled and spoilt now. Then she realised the shouting and commotion wasn't in her dream. It was actually happening in the corridor beyond her room. She crawled off the bed and padded over to the door. She crouched down and placed her ear to the door, trying to make out the shouts that seemed to echo around the first floor.

'She needs to be taught a lesson. Give me the key.' That was her brother.

'Damn him!' she muttered. What had she supposedly done now?

'Joseph! Be careful. Remember what happened last time!' That was her mother.

'I don't care. She's brought it all on herself. I should have broken the door down last night – she's lucky I didn't. She just walked out! I'll kill her!'

Genevieve stood up. She felt a thump on the door, followed by another thump and the mad rattling of the handle. Her heart beat faster and for the first time she felt scared. She knew what he was capable of. He had had a whole night to fester about whatever it was. She looked down at her dress and the memories flooded back. She felt slightly sick. Yes – there had been the ball, hadn't there? Oh, God. She'd left it, hadn't she? And Joseph wasn't going to wait any longer to punish her, that was for sure. She looked around her room. The only safe way out was through the window. She checked that the key was still in the lock and hurried over to her dressing table. She rifled through the drawers, grabbing a couple of things. She pulled a hooded cape out of her wardrobe and fastened it around herself. She pinned her hair up loosely and threw open the window. The cold air made her catch her breath and she leaned out to see if anybody was circling the gardens below. She would put nothing past her brother.

'Genevieve! Out of that room. Now!' he shouted. The door groaned on its hinges and her heart fluttered again. She had to go and she had to go now. She didn't know where to, and she didn't know for how long, but she knew she couldn't stay locked in her room. There was only one place she could think of. She prayed that he wouldn't have left yet.

Genevieve scrambled over the window ledge and stood on the tiny balcony that jutted out over the gardens. There had been a trellis there earlier in the year, but it was gone now, thanks to her brother. The old, gnarled branches of a climbing rose tree still clung onto the side of the house, thick stems of rosewood intertwining with strong, twisting ivy; she thought she might just manage it. The idea of rose thorns hooking into her flesh was preferable to what she would have to face from her brother if he caught her. She stepped over the balcony and grasped one of the ivy branches. The door to her bedroom rattled again and she heard her brother's raised voice. Thank goodness the locks were solid. She eased the rest of her body over the balcony and somehow managed to clamber down. She jumped the last few feet, landing awkwardly, but firmly. She ran around to the stables and quickly opened the door of Star's stall.

'Come on, girl,' she said and mounted the horse. She rode bareback, as Will had taught her years ago when they were children. She dug her heels into Star's flanks and turned the horse's head in the direction of Hartside; Will's home.

Genevieve didn't feel the cold. Star was warm beneath her and she knew the way to Hartside. Genevieve galloped across the moors, past the ruined chapel and tried to quash the thought of what had happened there in the summer. To be fair, it was more the thought of what had happened afterwards that she tried hard to forget – but that day was the one day that stood out quite clearly in her mind.

Will had met her there as usual and the chapel had been mellow in the sunlight with purple flowers trailing down the walls and green, velvety grass that seemed to wrap itself around the stones. She couldn't recall how it had all started, or how they had suddenly decided that the time was right and they wanted to explore every inch of each other's body. She remembered cloudless, blue sky and the scent of pollen and fresh grass. There was the nearby humming of a bee as it flitted from daisy to clover and back again and a sense of shock and realisation as her childhood playmate suddenly turned into a man and the object of her desire.

It should have been perfect. It would have been perfect, had she not discovered a few weeks later that she was carrying a child. She hadn't been the only one who learned that. Her brother had already guessed. He was waiting for her in the hallway. He had dragged her into his study and beat her until she confessed. He had beaten the whole story out of her: the place, the time, the father... Her mother had been outside the door, shouting, what seemed like encouragement, to him. She was a bad girl, a terrible daughter, a slut. By then, the room was spinning. Genevieve collapsed onto the floor and the world turned black. She assumed that she been had taken to her room afterwards. She woke up three days later, no longer pregnant and barely able to move without pain. It was a further week before she was allowed out of her room. During that time, Joseph had the trellis removed from the wall, just in case she tried to escape or Will tried to come in. Will had stayed away of course, and Genevieve was oddly pleased about that. He, at least, was safe. She discovered later that he had gone to London until the dust settled. Her bruises were written off as a 'riding accident' and the incident glossed over. It was horrendous that she knew the truth and could never tell anyone. It preyed on her already fragile mind. What was worse, she wondered – a riding accident or the pregnancy of an unmarried eighteen year old member of a respectable family? There was no option; she had to let the riding accident story spread. Genevieve knew, though, that the servants had no such compunction. They loved gossip; and they knew people in other houses who also loved gossip. Miss Genevieve's 'riding accident' was the talk of the county. Not once during that time did anyone ask her how she felt about it. She saw Will afterwards, eventually, at the chapel. She told him what had happened and never spoke of it again.

***

Genevieve cantered across the moors until the gates of Hartside appeared on the grey horizon. A flash of something caught her eye in a cluster of trees by Hartside. She glanced across at the woods and saw a black figure. She made a small noise in the back of her throat and dug her heels into the horse. If that was her brother, she was as good as dead.

'Oh, thank God!' she cried as she approached the house and saw that the gates were open. She raced through them, along the carriageway and up to the front door, pulling Star up at the steps. Dismounting, she stumbled up the steps and hammered on the door. It seemed like an age before it was answered. The door was barely ajar, and she was pushing her way through it. 'Where's Will? Where's Mr Hartley?' she shouted, running past the butler.

'Miss de Havilland!' cried Wheeler. 'Mr Hartley is...'

'He's gone? He's already left?' she shouted, swinging around to face the elderly man. 'When did he go? Can I reach him before he leaves the country?'

'Please, control yourself, Miss!' said the butler. 'Calm down! He hasn't left. He's in the drawing room.'

'I must see him!' cried Genevieve. Will was here, he would protect her. Everything would be all right. She ran across the hall to the doorway leading into the drawing room. She knew her way well.

'Miss Genevieve!' Wheeler snapped. 'You cannot go in there, the family have guests. I will have to find Sir Harold.' The butler turned and shuffled off to the other wing of the house, presumably to find Will's father.

Genevieve launched herself at the drawing room door and threw it open, bursting into the room. 'Will!' she cried. 'You have to help me! My brother...' she stopped short as two people turned to face the door at exactly the same moment. One was Will.

The colour drained from his face as he stared at her. 'Genevieve!' he said. 'What on earth are you doing here?'

She saw his eyes travel up and down her body, taking in the dishevelled hair, the ruined ballgown and the filthy satin slippers. Along with Will, was a small, slim girl, beautifully dressed in emerald green; she had clear, blue eyes framed by long, dark eyelashes. Her hair was a coppery colour, piled up onto her head with tendrils falling in loose waves onto her shoulders. She looked young and fresh-faced, her rosebud mouth a perfect 'o' as she stared at Genevieve.

'Will?' she asked. 'Who's this?' She continued staring at Genevieve.

'She's a friend of the family,' Will said, still looking at Genevieve. 'I'll deal with her, don't worry.' He moved towards Genevieve. 'Come on. Let's go into a different room.' He put his hand on her arm and Genevieve snatched it away.

Genevieve matched the girl's stares, her face thunderous. 'Who is *she*?' Genevieve demanded. 'How dare she ask who *I* am?'

'Excuse me!' said the girl. 'I have every right to ask. Will is my fiancé.'

***

Genevieve felt her precarious little world tilt on its axis. Fiancé? Will? Her Will? 'You lying...' she began, turning on the girl.

'No!' interjected the girl. 'Why would I lie about it? I met Will in the summer in London. He proposed to me and I accepted.

54

We are to be married next week. Will is about to travel back to Kent with me. I think you should leave now. Will doesn't need your kind of friendship anymore.'

The girl glared at Genevieve with such hatred that Genevieve felt something inside her snap. Nobody except her brother had ever regarded her like that and she was not going to take it from this stranger. She let out a cry which would have brought a lesser person to their knees and flew at the girl.

'Genevieve!' shouted Will. The strange girl jumped out of her chair and backed away. Will again tried to steer Genevieve out of the drawing room. 'I need to talk to you.'

'Oh no, Will Hartley, I don't think you do!' shouted Genevieve. Her voice dropped, dripping sarcasm. 'Does she know where you were last night? Does your fiancée know that?' She began to laugh. 'How ironic, Will. I'm not surprised you didn't want to take me with you on your travels.'

'Out! Now!' said Will. 'Cassandra, don't listen to her. We'll go into the...' He never finished his sentence, his words interrupted by a loud bang. The copper-haired girl began to scream as Will slumped to the floor, blood spurting from a wound in his chest. Genevieve stood over him shaking. A small, pearl-handled revolver was in her hand. She had brought it with her from the house, from her dressing table, where she had hidden it for the last few months. She had always intended using it on Joseph. She had brought it with her today for protection from him, should he choose to pursue her to Hartside.

'Ah Will,' said Genevieve, staring at him, half-wondering what he was doing on the floor. It had been extraordinarily quick, quite astonishing, really. 'Will, remember when you showed me how to use this little beauty?' she murmured. Then she turned to the strange girl who was terrified, panic and tears choking her as she cowered behind the piano. 'Your turn,' Genevieve said, quite calmly. She smiled sweetly and fired the pistol at her. The girl gasped, her eyes opened wide and she dropped to the floor. Genevieve stared for a moment, then came to her senses. She felt the gun in her hand; she saw two people lying on the floor. She felt the bile rise into her throat and the room began to swim.

Genevieve backed out of the room and heard footsteps pounding through the corridors. People had been alerted by the gun shots. She ran to the doorway, still clutching the gun and headed out

55

of the house. Star was waiting for her, looking confused and unsettled.

'Star – we have to go now! She cried and swung herself onto the horse. The white horse threw her head back and galloped out of the driveway.

***

As they left the gates of Hartside far behind, Genevieve suddenly realised that she was trapped. What was left for her now? Will had gone; even if she hadn't done...that... he was as good as dead to her. Genevieve couldn't go home. That was as good as suicide; she knew without a doubt that her brother would kill her.

She began to shake. '*It didn't happen,*' she told herself. '*It didn't happen. I didn't go there. He wasn't there...he's in London now.*' She almost managed, but part of her couldn't quite understand that she hadn't killed Will. Or his fiancée. She jolted back to reality as Star stopped at the ruined chapel.

'What is it Star? I don't think he's coming today,' she said. She dug her heels into Star's flanks again and tried to make her move, but the horse obstinately refused. Instead, she raised her head and gave a cautious whinny. Genevieve noticed a figure standing amongst the ruins. It walked across the chapel grounds towards her. Was it Joseph? Or Will? No, it was neither of them.

'So this is the chapel,' said Montgomery, looking about him. The building was grim and foreboding against the white landscape and Genevieve felt an unreasonable anger boil up inside her. She wanted to protect the place that she and Will had spent so much time in.

'You shouldn't be here,' she snapped. 'It's for Will and me. And besides, it doesn't look its best today. It's very drab. In the summer, you have beautiful...' her voice died, remembering the summer just gone. She felt sick and dizzy and the ruins began to blur out of focus. Damn Will! Damn him to Hell and back! Rage bubbled up inside her. Pure, evil, venomous rage. 'I hate him,' she said to no-one in particular. 'I hate him.' She turned to Montgomery and lifted her shoulders. 'I do. I hate him.'

Montgomery smiled. 'Nobody could speak of such a person or such a place with so much passion unless they had truly happy memories of being here, perhaps together,' he said.

'I did have good memories of this place,' said Genevieve with some surprise. 'Or at least, they used to be good memories.'

'Have the memories been tainted in some way?' pressed Montgomery.

Genevieve stared at the stained glass window wall. Was it really only yesterday she had seen Will here? 'I *did* have good memories,' she reiterated, 'but yes, my brother tainted them. I can't remember those feelings without remembering how it felt to have my brother's fist smashing into my face. And now there is nothing at all, nothing good. He has finally erased it all. Every last bit of it; everything.'

'Your brother?' asked Montgomery.

'Will Hartley,' murmured Genevieve, still staring at the stained glass window. 'He has spoiled it all. My brother would be so proud of him.'

'And what has Mr Hartley done?' asked Montgomery curiously. 'Surely, it can't be that bad. What could possibly have changed?'

'Oh! You think you know so much, yet you know so little,' said Genevieve. She dismounted and stumbled over to Montgomery. The cold and the shock were beginning to bite. 'Tell me, Sir, are all men alike?'

'It depends on what you are referring to,' said Montgomery. He touched his hand to her face and stared into her eyes. 'Has Mr Hartley dishonoured you? Has he cast you aside?'

'He has taken another lover.' Genevieve suddenly laughed. 'It's not even funny, is it? Yes, he's at present with a delightful young lady he met in London. Do you know, he ran off there? Yes, I nearly died at my brother's hands and my lover went to London and found himself a fiancée. Oh, forgive me, Sir Montgomery,' she said. 'I don't mean to speak ill of your dear friend. Dear Joseph.'

Montgomery shrugged. 'He is no friend of mine,' he said. 'I don't have friends.' He leaned closer to her and his eyes were dark in his pale face. 'What's happened? Can you confide in me at all?' He searched her face, trying, it seemed, to see into her very soul.

'He used to call me Veva,' she said. 'And this morning, he didn't.' She looked over Montgomery's shoulder, her mind's eye seeing the drawing room at Hartside once more. They would be coming soon, combing the moors, looking for her. They would know she was responsible. At least the snow was melting. Her tracks wouldn't be too visible. She felt in the small pocket of her cloak. Once it had contained little treasures like smooth stones or jewel-bright feathers Will had picked up for her when they were together. Now it held the instrument of his death. She could easily use it here; use it on herself, perhaps. She began to hum that strange little tune, just wondering what it would be like to die.

'Ah, there is something you aren't telling me,' said Montgomery.

'It's quite simple,' Veva said eventually. 'He's dead. I killed him. Oh, and I killed his fiancée. There. Now you know.' She flinched, half expecting him and even, dare she say it, wanting him to lash out at her and knock her to the ground. Her brother would have done that. Maybe if Montgomery did that, she would feel alive again. At this present moment in time, she was simply numb. Shouldn't she be screaming or still running away? She started pulling the pins out of her hair and dragging her fingers through it, agitated.

'I see,' said Montgomery watching her. He was calm, unruffled. 'Then I dare say he deserved it. I imagine you are feeling torn at the minute, unsure of which way to turn, perhaps?' He raised his hand and caught her hands in his. He lowered his face to hers and kissed her softly on the lips. 'I can perhaps help. He nuzzled into her neck, his skin even colder than hers. He pulled away and smiled at her. 'What's to stop us getting revenge in our own sweet way, my dear? Who's to stop us?'

The breath caught in her throat. 'What? Here? You're suggesting we..?'

'Why not?' asked Montgomery. 'I repeat, who is to stop us?'

'I just killed two people,' said Veva distractedly. 'I should be feeling something. I'm not.'

'Only two?' said Montgomery. 'You can do better than that. How about your brother? Isn't he on your list?' His eyes bored into her.

Veva stared back, mesmerised. 'Perhaps,' she said. She raised her face to Montgomery's, feeling his closeness, inhaling his scent. She released her hand from his and fingered the back of his cloak. 'I am very tempted, Sir,' she whispered, 'yet I fear we have little time. I think they're coming for me. Look – just over the brow of the hill. Can you see them?' She smiled a little and pulled away from him. She faced the dark shadows which were appearing over the horizon, her hair loose and rippling down her back. She relaxed her shoulders and held her head high. 'It will soon be over,' she said. 'You'd best leave. I might have enjoyed your company more under different circumstances.'

'I can stop them,' replied Montgomery. 'Or rather, I can stop them from hurting you.'

Veva shook her head, not taking her eyes off the oncoming horsemen. 'It's over. I'm ready to die, if that is what they intend,' she said. 'What's done is done.'

'You recall I told you I had to make some difficult decisions?' he said. 'Allow me to present you with your options.' He leant over her and whispered in her ear.

Veva's eyes widened and she turned to face him. 'Do it,' she said. 'Now.'

Montgomery smiled at Genevieve; a slow, thoughtful smile. 'Are you sure? You do understand the consequences?' he asked. 'Swear to me that you understand and only then shall I help you.'

'I understand perfectly,' she said. 'I have no choice. This way – your way – I can be free. I can disappear and leave them all. How long will it take?' She searched his face anxiously.

'A matter of seconds,' he said, taking hold of her shoulders. 'Then when they find you, you will no longer be of concern to them.'

'What will happen?' she asked slowly. The sounds of the horses' hooves were coming closer. 'Will you come and get me afterwards?'

'They have to see you – they have to believe. Then, once they are satisfied justice has been done, I would imagine they will leave you alone. When they return,' he shrugged, 'you will be gone.'

Genevieve fingered the gun and looked at the man before her. 'Do it,' she said again. He held his hand out and she passed the gun to him.

Swift as lightning, Montgomery leaned into Genevieve. If anyone had witnessed it, he would have appeared to have been kissing her. The girl let out one gasping scream and slumped forwards, her eyes closed. The man caught her and laid her gently on an old, box-like tomb. Then he raised the gun and shot her through the heart.

***

There was blood, of course, a lot of blood. When they found her, the gun was in her hand, her fingers loosely curled around the trigger; a clear case of murder-suicide. The girl had been unbalanced, they knew that. Her family had made that obvious and her recent

59

behaviour had proved it. They stood over her body, wondering what to do. She was evil, a murderess. There was no motive except her insanity.

One of the men stared at her and shook his head. 'We're too late,' he said. 'We have to go back and tell the Master. Do we take her with us?'

Another man looked at him in horror. 'Take that back to the Master?' he said, indicating the bloodied body. 'No. We tell him what we saw. Then he can come down here himself if he wants to see it. Do we tell her family?'

'No. We tell our Master first,' said another. 'He's the one that needs to know.' They took a last look at Genevieve de Havilland. 'God only knows what evil was hiding behind that face,' muttered the first man. 'Come on. We should go.' They turned and mounted their horses again, urging the animals away from the chapel, back towards Hartside.

***

Montgomery came out from behind the pillar where he had been standing. Nobody had realised he was there; that was one benefit, he thought, of a half-life such as his. He could fool them into thinking he was invisible at times. He walked over to Veva and leaned over her. He pushed her hair back and studied the two deep marks in her neck. Blood had poured down from the gash where he had severed her jugular, soaking the front of her dress and, mingled with the mess of the bullet wound in her chest; a layman might assume that the blood all came from the bullet wound. He stood up and lifted the girl gently in his arms. He wouldn't have to wait long before she was with him again, but she was a wild one, no doubt about it. A gust of wind blew down the moor and snow began to fall from the heavy clouds above; he didn't feel any of it. He half smiled again. He didn't envy her brother when she woke up.

***

There was a cottage on the moors, an abandoned, estate-worker's cottage hidden behind a small clump of trees. It was fairly dry inside. Montgomery didn't care about heat or warmth; Veva wouldn't either, when she woke up. He shouldered the door open and walked inside. There were two rooms which led off from a small, stone passageway. Montgomery went into the room on the right and laid the girl down on the one remaining wooden bench by the inglenook fireplace. He sat opposite her to wait.

There was no gentle stirring from her. She moved her head and her eyes snapped open, staring straight at him. Her expression was shocked and confused for a split second, but then she smiled at him, slowly and triumphantly. Even being what he was, and knowing what he knew, Montgomery still experienced a shiver of trepidation as he looked into the girl's eyes.

'You did it,' she said. 'Did they see me?'

Montgomery nodded. 'They did indeed,' he said. 'Your fate was sealed. Your body has been moved, you are dead to them. You are no longer their concern.'

Veva sat up carefully. She looked about her, and her eyes rested on the front of her ballgown. A bloodied, burnt hole scarred the blue fabric at her breast. 'My beautiful dress!' she cried 'Oh no!' She pressed her hand to her chest. 'Did you shoot me? I can feel something...'

'It will soon heal over,' said Montgomery. 'We don't sustain our injuries for very long.'

'I'm glad I shot them,' she said. 'Now, there is more work I need to do.' She swung her legs over the side of the bench and stood up unsteadily.

Montgomery reached out to take her hand, gently yet firmly stopping her. 'Not yet,' he said. 'You need to gain strength, my love. You're still weak. Let your body heal and your mind adjust.'

Veva narrowed her eyes and turned to Montgomery. She wrenched her hand out of his and snarled at him. 'You think that you are the one who can tell me what to do now, is that it? No. You have given me independence. I can do what I want now, but I need to settle some old scores first.'

'I am not telling you what to do,' said Montgomery, 'I am advising you to rest. Your body has gone through an ordeal and it may take some time to recover.'

'I went through worse this summer at the hands of my brother. I died, you know. They told me. But then I came back. Joseph did not know whether to be grateful or resentful. I am sure he wished me dead.' She smiled. 'Dear Joseph. He did his best. Sadly, it was not enough to stop me. I must pay him a visit.'

Montgomery sighed. 'Go then, Genevieve. Go and see him. I can see that I have no power over you to prevent it. I would have visited him myself, but why should I rob you of the experience? All I will say is that if you rest now, you will be stronger. Look, you are still

61

unsteady on your feet. Please – an hour, two hours at the most. That will be enough time for you. It will be enough time for the message to reach him as well. Would it not be better to visit him from a position of such strength in two hours time, than to go now and risk more people seeing you as the news of your apparent suicide spreads? You have much to learn and I can teach you, but the first step is to trust me.'

Veva paused in the doorway of the cottage, looking thoughtfully at Montgomery. 'You tell me that I will be stronger if I wait?' she asked.

'Indeed,' he replied. 'I found it best to wait.'

'Why did you make this choice?' asked Veva curiously. She walked across to him and stared down at him thoughtfully. 'What was it that you did?'

'I made many mistakes in life,' replied Montgomery. 'I inherited a failing estate. I had no business acumen. I begged people like your brother to help me. I did not necessarily want the money, but I would have appreciated the support. He, amongst others, laughed at my disgrace and sent me away. I decided that my only chance was to gamble with the few remaining shreds of my fortune, and I lost. I remember sitting in a dark room, with nothing left to my name except a few coins in my hand, wondering how I could kill myself painlessly. I wandered through the streets of London that night, intending to throw myself into the river. I saw a lady in the shadows, and decided to spend my money on her before I finished it for good. I found myself telling her what had happened. She offered me a way out – a new way of life where I could start again and would not have to rely on mortal fortune to feed me or shelter me. I was desperate. So I made my choice. I shall not go into how I recovered my money - and more - from the men I gambled with. Suffice it to say, I felt vindicated. Thus, I returned to my family estate where I live quite alone, apart from the occasional visit from a housekeeper who knows better than to ask any questions.'

Veva nodded. 'I see. Then, if you advise me to wait, I shall wait. I shall wait for two hours and no longer. Tell me, Sir. How do you think we should pass the time?'

Montgomery stood up, that half-smile playing across his lips again. 'I think you know the answer to that, my little wild one,' he said and cupped her face in his hands. 'Veva, you are perfect.'

Veva smiled and drew closer to him as the clouds gathered in the sky and the day began to darken over the ruined chapel. 'I think I *shall* let you call me Veva,' she whispered, 'just this once.'

'And you, my love,' he replied, 'can call me Guy.'

***

It is a myth that vampires do not rest. They sleep as most creatures do and when Montgomery awoke, it was to find Veva gone. He knew where she would have gone: and he felt no remorse over it. He smiled into the darkness; there was no need for him to linger here any longer. He would leave immediately. First, he stretched across to where his cloak lay abandoned on the ground. He felt around the inside pocket and his fingers closed over the object he sought; the silver dagger he had stolen from the girl in London, the first night of his new life. He had no idea what it was for – vaguely, he remembered, he had wondered if he would need some sort of security, just in case. Just in case the killing didn't come easily. Just in case he didn't succeed in reclaiming his fortune. Just in case. At least Veva hadn't found that. She had obviously been eager to leave.

'Rest in peace, Joseph de Havilland,' Sir Guy Montgomery murmured. 'I'm pleased that she is the one who will do it. You deserve no less.'

***

Veva didn't quite know what drew her back to the house after she left Montgomery. She needed to be certain in her own mind. Had Will died, then? She wasn't sure any more. She wondered what she would do if someone saw her? Well – the answer was simple. She would kill them. She crept around the outside of the house like a shadow. She wanted to look into the drawing room and remember Will, remember how he had been with her. Maybe he was still there. But now she had spent the night with Montgomery, she realised just how different her times with Will had been. She had felt more detached with Montgomery, had concentrated more on her pleasure than his. It had been very different with Will. There was a fine line, she realised, between love and hate. She had loved Will desperately, but had hated him with a passion when she pulled the trigger. Oh – so maybe he *was* dead? She frowned. It was easier to hate the girl than to ponder on the mechanics of the situation. Cassandra - that was what she was called. Veva felt the anger bubble up inside her as she pressed herself close to the wall and melted into the brickwork, listening for any activity inside. Her senses were alive: she buzzed with the stimulation around her, noises were magnified and her eyes saw things so much more clearly, she wondered how she had possibly managed before. She stopped suddenly, looking upwards to an open bedroom window. She wrinkled her nose. She could smell blood – metallic and sharp, yet underlined with a sickly sweetness. She heard ragged breathing from the room, a shallow stuttering and gurgling coming from someone who obviously lay there. Her first thought was of Will. Was he still alive? She straightened up and stared at the window. No. He couldn't be. Not the way she had hit him, full force in the chest with the bullet. The girl, then - could it be...? No. No, she didn't want to think about her surviving. The anger enveloped her again and she narrowed her eyes, listening carefully.

The walls of the house were a rough hewn stone. Veva stood back a little, assessing them. She reached out her fingers, running them across the bricks, searching for crevasses and cracks in the mortar. She tensed her body and with her finger-tips somehow curling into the niches, she began to scale the wall. She proceeded cautiously at first, then her confidence grew and she clambered up until she was able to quietly prise the casement open and peer through the gap.

It *was* the girl. She lay in a pristine white bed, her coppery hair spread out around her. Veva made a small growling sound in her throat and pushed the window open further, just enough to ease her way inside the gap and land silently on the polished wooden floorboards. She moved across to the bed and stared at the girl. She knew instinctively what she needed to do and leaned over her.

'I can't let you live, you know that don't you?' she muttered to the unresponsive figure on the bed. 'I should have made sure before...'

***

Joseph de Havilland stood in the ruins of the chapel looking at the table tomb where they said her body had been found. He could see that she had been there; her blood had soaked into the old grey stone and run down the sides of it, seeping into the grass where it stained the slush a dark rust colour. They had told him yesterday what had happened. At first he hadn't believed it and had raged at them all. Then, when he had demanded to be taken to Hartside, he had seen Will's body and realised that his sister had killed her lover.

He shouldn't have been surprised. It was in them all. Older than Genevieve, Joseph had copied his behaviour from his father.

His father had taken his own life as well – they had passed it off as a hunting accident with a shot gun. What was it about guns? How had his sister acquired that one? And, more importantly, why? Joseph's blood chilled a little as he processed the thought. He had a good idea why. Well. He was safe now. Her death was a relief. He knew he had gone too far in the summer, and she had constantly chipped away at him since, threatening to tell the truth. She had earned several beatings since by pushing him to his limit. Why would she never learn? He was willing to bet she had told Will Hartley the truth; he was relieved that he was dead as well. Now the family could erase the pair of them from their lives and move on.

But it was a mystery where the body had gone, he pondered. Maybe a wild animal had taken her? That was preposterous. No. He didn't know where the body had gone, but someone must have taken it. He would make more enquiries in the village, but deep down he recoiled at the fact that he would be expected to wax lyrical at her funeral; to pretend that they had actually cared about one another as siblings were supposed to. No, he wouldn't be in a rush, he thought, to locate Genevieve.

The sun was setting low over the hills and he shivered. The snow had turned a pinkish colour on the horizon, shadowed with purple and lilac. Joseph heard the strange silence that comes with a winter's evening, and he felt the loneliness of the moors and the fact that there was nothing around him for miles. Hartside was to the North and the Hall was to the South. He was dead centre, Joseph thought, right in the middle of two households that had dealt with death and violence in the last twenty four hours. The thought unsettled him. It was Genevieve's fault, of course. The selfish bitch had given no thought to those who would have to clear up her mess. He set his lips, anger building up within him. Even in death, she was mocking him, making him suffer for her actions.

Joseph became aware of a humming nearby, a soft, slightly off-key aria that he recognised as being one of the tunes Genevieve used to pick out on the piano. He whipped his head around to the direction it seemed to be coming from and saw nothing. Then he heard a quiet laugh. He shivered again, shaking his head. He was imagining things. She was always there, always in his head. He would never have any peace from her - never. He heard the laugh again, closer this time, and spun round. He caught sight of a pale blur against the darkness of the church columns and it seemed to drift towards him in the half-light.

'What the..?' he cried.

The laugh came again, and a voice began to recite some words from a popular novel. '"The yellow glamour of the sunset, clothed in transparent radiance,"' it said, '"this shadowy revenant from the tomb." From the book *John Inglesant: A Romance*, by Joseph Henry Shorthouse. You tried to make me read that, do you remember? You tried to instil some worthy religious ideas into my poor, wicked head. I only ever liked that line. I loved that image. I wanted to rise from my tomb, a shadowy revenant which would haunt you for evermore. Have I succeeded? Dearest brother, don't look so surprised. I came back from the dead once before, did I not? But maybe you did not expect to see me again this time. Have I upset you? Poor, *poor* brother. I didn't mean to.'

The figure came closer to Joseph and he gasped. Before him was Genevieve, clothed in her tattered, bloodied ballgown from days ago, just standing and smiling at him. Her eyes were black and her skin alabaster and Joseph could not read the expression on her face. It was triumphant, complacent, even - yet pure evil radiated from her.

'Genevieve? You're alive? They said...' Joseph tailed off. The girl came closer and Joseph's heart began to pound.

'No, I'm not alive, brother. Neither am I dead.' She dropped her voice. 'I am the substance of nightmares,' she whispered, 'your nightmares. I really don't know how to do this. You'll be my first proper kill and the one I will remember for the rest of my long, wonderful existence. You can't hurt me now, Joseph. But I wonder - how shall I kill you? Hmmm.' She tilted her head on one side and appraised him. Joseph began to shake. He turned and tried to run, but she was in front of him. She laughed. 'You can't escape. So don't even try.'

'Genevieve! It's a chapel...'

'*Deconsecrated!*' she fired back. 'I told you. You will die here, Joseph. I just need to choose the best way. I want you to suffer. And I want to enjoy it. I want to know how you felt all those times you attacked me. I want to know what is so awe-inspiring about hurting people, about bringing them so close to death...so, so close. And above all, I want to know what made you *continue to do it!*' Joseph stumbled backwards as she screeched the last few words, her face inches from his.

'You killed Will!' he shouted. 'You don't need to use me...'

It was the wrong thing to say. With a cry that froze the blood in his veins, Veva lashed out and dragged her nails across his face, tearing the skin from his cheek. He saw her eyes widen and her lips draw back over her teeth. As she threw herself at him and crashed him to the ground, the last thing he heard was laughter, ringing out around the old ruined chapel.

Present Day

'So where do you want to start?' asked Drew. He pushed his hands in his pocket and stared around the street. 'We have to go to a pub. We have to get wasted the first night. It's the law.'

'Well, the town centre – if that's what you can call it - seems to be that way,' said Lucas. He nodded up the street, and Drew looked in the direction he indicated.

'Yeah, that's where they all seem to be heading,' he replied. A stream of people were meandering up the road. Lucas watched a middle aged couple dressed in matching jerseys and walking boots go past. He couldn't tell if they were holiday makers or locals. But it was a fair bet they were heading to the pub.

'Come on, then,' he said to Drew. 'Let's go.' He wondered if he'd see that Cass there tonight. He also wondered exactly how many pubs were on the island. They had all assumed the hotels would have bars too, but the flip side of that, was that the hoteliers might frown on a group of lads landing on them. Alex had said they were probably used to it and some of them had already gone off towards one of the bigger hotels. Lucas and Drew had mock-saluted them and wished them luck.

The two boys headed up the street, following the walking-boot couple. Soon they could hear laughter and music coming from a building on the corner and they high-fived one another.

'Result,' said Drew and hurried on ahead. The wind was blowing up and there were a few spots of rain. Lucas could taste the salt in the air and he shivered. It was a nice place, but the tide had covered the causeway now and he suddenly understood exactly how marooned they were. Drew pushed the door open and the warmth and the smell of beer assailed them. It was a welcome contrast to the chill outside.

'What you having?' asked Drew and pushed through the crowds to the bar without waiting for an answer. Lucas watched him get swallowed up by the people and saw his head moving along as he jiggled from left to right: Drew swore that it made the bar staff notice you more than pushing forward like everyone else did. Lucas looked around the pub and spotted three of his friends in a corner. They waved him across and he turned to go towards them when he felt a soft pressure on his arm. The red-head from the fence was there next to him.

'Hello, Lucas,' she smiled. 'I thought I'd find you here.'

'Cass!' he said. 'Well – it is a small island and there can't be many places to go to of an evening, I guess.'

'You'd be surprised,' she said. 'I know plenty. Did you go to the lime kilns?'

'Not yet,' he said. 'I saw them advertised in the B&B. I thought I might try them tomorrow.'

'I could come with you?' she said. 'I think it's best to have a guide, don't you?'

'I don't know,' replied Lucas. 'It depends on what there is to see there.'

'A local person would be the best to explain that to you, in my opinion,' laughed Cass. She paused for a moment. 'Oh, really, Lucas, do I have to spell it out to you?' Lucas knew she was flirting with him; he fingered his mobile unconsciously.

'Ahhhh,' she said. 'I understand. What's she called?'

'What's who called?' asked Lucas.

'Your girlfriend. Look, come on outside with me. It's too noisy in here.' She drew her eyebrows together and pulled a face. 'I can't stand it!' Lucas looked across at his friends. Drew had by now been served and was pushing his way over to the table with the rest of the lads. He looked up and caught Lucas' eye. He grinned and winked and lined the two pints up in front of him. He sat down with his back pointedly to Lucas and leaned over to speak to Jared. Lucas knew he had effectively been dismissed.

'OK,' he said, half-reluctantly. Cass laughed and took his hand. She pulled him gently out of the pub and they walked out onto the street. A gust of wind bit into him and he shivered.

'I live over there,' Cass said, pointing to a stone cottage set a little way apart from the village. 'Well, I don't live there permanently. I travel a lot. My sister and I rented it so we'd have a base to come back to. It's nice. It's not quite a home; but it's not quite a holiday home either. We're left to our own devices mainly. We don't bother the Islanders and they don't bother us.'

'I guess it must be hard to fit in here,' Lucas said, more for the sake of conversation than anything else.

'Not really,' she said. 'As I say, we don't bother the people who live here. If they started prying into our lives, well, maybe we would reconsider.' She laughed again. 'They think my sister is a bit

69

odd. That's the truth of it. I couldn't tell her that though. She'd never speak to me again.'

'What do you mean by odd?' asked Lucas. He shivered again as another gust of wind blew down the street.

Cass laughed and rubbed his bare arm. 'No coat. Silly boy. I can tell you're a southerner. With Jenny, I think it's just because people don't understand her. She's very...creative. I think that's part of it. She's hard work at times. I try not to get involved. Or she would lose her temper with me and seriously, it's not worth it!' She looked over to the cottage again. 'I'd take you there tonight, but she's in a funny mood. I want to enjoy some time with you first. So tell me about your girlfriend then.'

'My girlfriend?' asked Lucas. The statement caught him off his guard.

'You were fiddling with your mobile phone,' said Cass. 'That means you were expecting a call or a text. And you fiddled with it when I asked you to the lime kilns. Regardless, you'll get nothing here. You might as well leave it in the hotel. No signal – anywhere. But still, you're undecided about what to do. What's your girlfriend called?'

'Laura,' said Lucas. 'I mean, she *was* my girlfriend, but I don't think she is any more.' He smiled wryly.

Cass watched him, her eyes bright in the semi-darkness. 'What's so funny?' she asked, a slight edge creeping into her voice. 'Why is it funny that she's not your girlfriend anymore?'

'It's not! It's not funny at all,' said Lucas. 'Sorry.'

'What did you do to upset her?' asked Cass. She had folded her arms.

'It was a mistake – that's all,' he replied. Why on earth was he justifying himself to this girl? The memory of that night out a couple of months ago still left him cold. It was one of those cheap trebles nights at his local – very dangerous. He had bumped into Irina, the stunningly beautiful Russian girl from the espresso bar. She'd come up to him and they'd been talking and one thing led to another. They'd bought each other different vodkas to try and ended up staggering back to his place. It was only one night. He wasn't even sure whether anything had happened; he woke up and she'd gone. Two weeks later he had been mortified to find her crying outside his house.

'I ees pregnant,' she had said. 'Eet is yours.' Laura was with him at the time. She screamed and yelled and, quite rightly, told him it was over.

Too late, he had discovered that Irina had tried the same trick on two of his other friends; she eventually admitted the father was her married boss. Irina had disappeared shortly after that. Someone said they'd seen her working in a restaurant on the other side of town, her bump just beginning to show beneath her apron. Simple maths told Lucas – and his friends – it wasn't possible for them to be anything to do with the baby. Laura, although accepting this, still wouldn't forgive him for what might or might not have happened that night. Lucas heard on the grapevine that Laura was even more disgusted with Irina for drinking when she knew she was pregnant. Laura was a trainee nurse and she knew all the risks. Lucas had vaguely hoped this would put him in a better light; Irina's actions were clearly the act of a desperate young girl. But Laura didn't see it like that.

He didn't want to tell this Cass his life story though. He shrugged. 'It's ancient history. It's well over,' he said.

'But it was your fault?' pressed Cass.

'I suppose so,' said Lucas.

Cass suddenly laughed. 'Well that's good. You've at least admitted responsibility. And it's over with you and this...Laura,' she said the girl's name with such distaste Lucas was momentarily shocked. 'So...' Suddenly, Cass was at his side. She ran her fingers up his bare arm again and he felt the hairs stand up on end. Her voice was almost a purr as she continued speaking. 'The coast is clear for me then?'

Lucas stared at her. 'If you put it like that...' he began.

Cass tilted her head up and kissed him quickly. 'Excellent,' she replied. She opened her mouth to speak and a voice, seemingly carried on the wind, called her name.

'Cass...'

Cass spun around and made an annoyed noise in her throat. 'Jenny,' she said. 'What are you doing here?' Lucas peered through the ever-darkening evening and saw a tall, slim figure appear out of a pathway between two houses. The figure walked into a pool of light cast by a streetlamp and Lucas caught his breath. *Bloody Hell, if that's the sister, the family genes must be good*, he thought.

The girl stared at him and smiled shyly. 'Hello,' she said. 'I see you've met Cass.' She walked towards Lucas and held her hand out in a funny, formal sort of way. She had a curtain of dark hair, parted at the side just above her ear. A clip or slide of some description clumped it together on the opposite side to her parting where it tumbled down past her shoulders. The whole effect was of a dishevelled beauty that had just woken up. She blinked huge eyes at Lucas and smiled slowly. 'I'm Jenny.'

'Hello,' he said, holding his hand out to her. She took it firmly, which surprised him somewhat. She looked like such a fragile thing.

'We live over there.' Jenny pointed at the cottage.

'I know, Cass has already told me,' replied Lucas.

'Jenny, we should probably go home,' interrupted Cass. 'It's late.'

'I don't mind,' said Jenny. She never took her eyes off Lucas. 'I think I like you,' she said to him. She laughed. 'What's he called, Cass?'

'This is Lucas,' replied Cass. 'I was just getting to know him better.'

'Oh? Well now, I think I'd like to get to know him as well,' she said.

Cass took hold of her sister's shoulders and physically moved her away from Lucas. 'Not tonight,' said Cass. She turned to Lucas. 'I'm sorry,' she whispered. 'I'll take her home. The offer still stands for tomorrow, by the way. I'll be at the kilns about five. I'll see you there? Oh- what I said about the phone. She'll not text you. No signal. You might as well just leave it behind tomorrow.' She pushed her sister back towards the alleyway, none too gently. 'Goodnight. Sorry again.'

'No worries,' said Lucas and he watched the girls disappear into the night. Well now, it seemed true what Cass had told him. Jenny was indeed 'rather odd'. But she was also fascinating, in a strange sort of way. He wouldn't mind getting to know both of them a little better. After all - he fingered his phone again - Laura was off the scene for good now, wasn't she? There was still a little pang when he thought of her though. But it was, he had to admit, getting easier.

'You all right, mate?' shouted Drew's voice from the pub doorway. He'd obviously popped out for a cigarette - he claimed he was just a social smoker. 'Where's she gone? You coming back in or what?'

'Yeah. Just coming,' shouted Lucas. He looked into the darkness towards the cottage and thought he could make out two black shadows gliding through the darkened fields. The girls, on their way home. Cass was gorgeous, no doubt about it, but that Jenny, she was something else.

'Two of them?' cried Drew. 'Bloody Hell, mate! How do you do it?'

'Just one of them,' replied Lucas. But he'd be hard-pressed to decide which one, if it came down to it.

In the long, hot June of 1887, the streets of Britain were party to Golden Jubilee Celebrations for Her Majesty, Queen Victoria, Empress of India. The other major news story was the murder of Miriam Angel in Batty Street, London. It was astonishing how, in the space of one week, the emotions in the City could change from joy to horror as the details of the young woman's death were publicised; six months pregnant and apparently being forced to imbibe nitric acid by a gentleman lodger was not a favourable way to die.

Veva sat in the morning room flicking through the *Penny Illustrated Paper* and smiling to herself. 'We should try that,' she murmured, 'that would be an excellent way to dispose of a person.' Her beautiful face hardened. 'Although, it does prove that men are still of the opinion that women exist only to be used.' She received no response to her comment and looked up. She frowned. Cassandra was staring out of the window again. Veva could tell by the set of her shoulders that she was desperate to be outside, amongst the crowds. The girls had acquired a small townhouse just off Fenchurch Street. It was perfect for them; much better, Veva had suggested, than it had been for the previous occupant. He had just disappeared one day, she told a curious neighbour. He had been their Uncle. It was terrible for the whole family, although the girls had been granted permission to use the house whilst they waited for the rest of their family to arrive. The sisters had been passing through Surrey, you see, so it wasn't too far for them to travel. Shortly after that, the neighbour had disappeared too.

From Fenchurch Street, the girls could slip through Aldgate and lose themselves in the grimy, poverty-stricken East End. They could also head west into the more pleasant parts of the City. In addition, the house was not far away from the train station, and there were often people passing through that area of London. It was terribly easy for travellers, they realised, to disappear in such a seething capital. Veva didn't miss her old life, but it was clear that Cassandra was not as settled.

'I want to go out tonight,' said Cassandra. 'It's been too long.'

'Sweetheart, we went out last week,' said Veva.

'No, we did not go out. We went to the river and met that couple.'

Veva shrugged. 'I suspected that he was married. Why else would he be under the bridge with her? We did the right thing.'

'We did,' agreed Cassandra, turning away from the window, 'but it wasn't enough.'

'Darling, you will never be Lillie Langtry,' laughed Veva. She stood up and reached across Cassandra's head, drawing the curtains firmly. 'You may wish to haunt the dance-halls and the theatres and hope that someone will take pity on you and invite you to perform, but they never will. You gave up every chance of that lifestyle, remember? You might be able to seduce the stage-hand one day, but you would end up killing him, and what use would that be?'

'I did not give up the lifestyle,' growled Cassandra. 'You made that decision for me.'

Veva shrugged. 'Perhaps.'

'I could have performed,' said Cassandra, balling up her fists, 'but no, Will proposed. I had to accept...'

'You did *not* have to accept!' shouted Veva. 'How many times do I have to tell you?'

'Veva! We've had this discussion before...

'*Don't* call me that!' yelled Veva. She lashed out to slap Cassandra, but the girl dodged out of the way, her reflexes fast. She had learned the hard way over the past two years. 'Two people have called me that in my entire life,' continued Veva. 'You are *not* to make it three, do you hear me?'

'Oh, yes. One was Sir Guy – I must thank him for this most humbly if I ever see him,' said Cassandra, curtseying mockingly. 'And who was the other one...ahh yes. Will. My fiancé.'

Veva flew at her and knocked her to the ground. 'Do you seriously think he preferred you?' she breathed, holding her down. 'Seriously?'

Cassandra opened her mouth to retaliate. Before she could answer, Veva drew her lips back and snarled. Cassandra gathered her strength together and pushed the dark-haired girl off her. Veva collapsed onto the floor, glaring at Cassandra. 'He was mine, you know,' she said. Her face suddenly went blank. 'If I ever find out who killed him, I might have to kill them myself,' she said thoughtfully. She sat on the floor and watched Cassandra straighten up and smooth her coppery hair down. Cassandra glared at Veva contemptuously. The girl's hair was tangled, hanging in dark waves down past her shoulders where the combs had come undone and she made no move to tidy herself up.

Veva smiled at Cassandra. 'You are actually quite pretty you know,' she said. She stood up and took a lock of Cassandra's hair between her fingers. 'You have hair like Lizzie Sidall. She died of laudanum poisoning. Do you think they ever wondered what happened to you at Hartside? Didn't they have laudanum by your bedside? Oh, I say,' she said, coming back to the present. 'Why don't we go out tonight?'

Cassandra slapped her hand away. 'I already suggested that,' she said.

'Did you, darling?' asked Veva, opening her eyes wide. 'Fancy that. What a marvellous idea.' Then she smiled, dropping the lock of hair. 'I wonder whether I'll see Will at the ball? That would be nice. Do you know Will? He's going to marry me, you know.' Veva laughed and turned away, drifting into the hallway singing to herself. Cassandra stared at her, infuriated. Would it never end?

***

'If I am right,' said Veva, 'I do believe that we should head west tonight, perhaps towards the Criterion Theatre?' She had clearly forgotten the incident from earlier. Cassandra was not going to remind her. 'You like the theatre, don't you?' she said, smiling at Cassandra. Cassandra glared at her. Veva blinked at her innocently, her features utterly perfect. 'What's wrong?' she asked. 'We don't have to go, you know. Here, let me do your hair for you. It might make you feel better.'

Cassandra moved out of the way as Veva reached over to her. 'Thank you, but no,' she said. It had taken her too long, brushing her auburn hair out until it shone and pinning it up onto the top of her head in a complicated arrangement of curls for Veva to spoil it.

Veva tutted. Her hair was never dressed as carefully as Cassandra's. Cassandra knew that the only thing she had to recommend her next to Veva, was her hair. Comparing the two girls, although they were both dazzling, Veva had the edge. There was just something more perfect about her face than Cassandra's, something that everybody was entranced by. Cassandra was not unaware of the situation. She had never thought that she would ever have to compete with someone for eternity the way she seemed to be destined to do with Veva. It was always what Veva wanted to do, always what Veva decided...

'Anyway,' Veva said, 'we should go soon. The crowds will be leaving and I think we need to find an after-show ball to attend, don't you?' Cassandra watched Veva tweak at her sky-blue ballgown and adjust a loop on the front where the overskirt was attached to the waist. She flipped the train out behind her, looked over her shoulder to check the bustle and posed by the fireplace. Cassandra didn't know if she'd ever hated anybody as much as she did in that moment. She looked down at her own oyster pink silk and smoothed the skirt down. She knew she was beautiful. But it was when they stood together, that she was conscious that everyone looked at Veva. Deep down, she couldn't help wondering whether Will Hartley had agreed to settle for less when he'd proposed to her. She had a feeling he was just like water – always taking the path of least resistance. She often wondered that, should things have turned out differently, would she have always have taken second place to Veva? A more rational Veva, perhaps, who would have become Will's mistress and flaunted it for all to see? She looked again at the dark-haired girl. No. Veva would never have settled for being his mistress; she would, without a doubt, have killed them both regardless.

***

Electric lights had replaced the gas lights in London and as the girls strolled the three miles or so towards the Criterion, Cassandra couldn't help being astounded by them. One thing she had to thank Veva for, was the fact that she now had the chance to experience so much more of the future. She would remain, frozen in time, as a beautiful, young girl with the world at her feet. She flirted with the idea of eventually being able to perform somehow. What was to stop her, after all? Then she caught the scent of a crowd of theatregoers and started to walk towards them. She felt Veva's hand on her arm, pulling her back.

'No, darling,' Veva said. She nodded at the crowd and walked past them. 'You've still got a little way to go, Cassandra,' she murmured. 'You're not quite ready to face the world on your own yet. We can't draw attention to ourselves like that.'

'I only wanted to see what the program said,' snapped Cassandra.

Veva shook her head. 'I don't think that's all you had in your mind,' she replied. 'Oh! See this – there appears to be a ball here. Come on, I think we've been invited. Oh no,' she pouted. 'I seem to have forgotten my invitation.' She sighed. 'Not to worry.'

77

She cast her eyes amongst the crowd. Plenty of people to wander amongst; there was bound to be some good sport to be found here.

Cassandra hung back. She could see the Criterion from here. 'Why can't we try the theatre first?' she asked.

'Because we are going to the ball,' replied Veva. She walked confidently up to the door of a large house and looked at the doorman earnestly. 'My sister and I have been invited, but I'm terribly sorry – we forgot our invitations.'

She looked so sad that the doorman did what they usually did. 'Well, Miss, on this occasion, I think we can probably allow you in,' he said. 'I can't imagine anyone not wanting to see you tonight.' He smiled and bowed and opened the door.

Veva's smile lit up her face. 'You are a lovely man,' she said. She turned to Cassandra who was scowling behind her. 'Isn't he nice, Sister? We should remember that later.' Cassandra did not reply. The girls disappeared into the house, Cassandra trailing behind, and they stood watching the people mill around. The house was bigger than it had appeared from the outside and the hallway was decorated with dozens of candles. Something shifted in Veva's face as she remembered another ball, some time ago, where the hallway was exactly the same. The shutters came down and she disappeared somewhere inside herself.

'Perfect,' she said. 'Just perfect. I would lay my life on the fact that he will come and see me tonight - how very exciting.'

***

Not far away, a young man with fair hair watched the crowds leave the theatres of the West End. He held himself well and attracted many admiring glances from the ladies. It was far nicer, he thought, watching people in this area than it was further east. The east of the City held some odd memories for him. That was where he had met the woman who had transformed his life. Sir Guy Montgomery had left London, headed back to his debt-ridden estate and went about settling his debts in very satisfying ways. It hadn't taken long for the estate to turn around, and that was when he had met Genevieve de Havilland. He often wondered what had happened to her. Still, she had not been a pet to be cosseted over, or even a child to be educated. She had been experimental; and in truth, he was a little horrified by what she had done to her brother. Although he felt no sympathy for the man, his demise held a sick fascination which had made Montgomery wonder just what else Veva was capable of.

78

'Good evening, Guy,' said a woman approaching him. She wore a scarlet gown and had jet black hair. Her eyes were green, the irises rimmed slightly with a scarlet that matched her clothing.

Guy reached out and smiled, taking her hand. He bowed over it and stood up. 'Good evening, Clara,' he said. 'It's an honour to see you tonight. I felt the need for a little fresh air; I am so pleased you accepted my invitation.'

The woman smiled. 'My pleasure,' she said. 'Are you sure you didn't feel the need for anything else tonight? I'm rather hungry, myself.' She scanned the crowd, as if she was assessing them for the kill.

'Perhaps later,' smiled Guy. 'You know, I would like to see the play first. The West End holds a certain appeal for me.'

'But the East End is better for meals,' replied Clara.

'You are, of course, correct,' smiled Guy, 'although I don't go there unless I have to.'

'Quite,' said Clara. 'Well, I suppose I could wait a little longer if you promise to look after me tonight.'

Guy smiled. Clara was an acquaintance he had met after the Genevieve disaster. She had lived her half-life since 1832 and was well versed in civilised behaviour. It was now the accepted thing that, whenever he was in London, they would visit a show and go hunting together. It was a guilty pleasure, perhaps, but who was there to tell Guy it was wrong? His lifestyle was of his own choosing. It did not harm the relationship when Guy discovered that Clara was an expert in love-making – she had learned it well over the years and enjoyed putting it into practice. She wasn't even sure if she had made love to the Prince; it might have been him, she had laughed, although she couldn't swear to it.

'It's very interesting what one hears within society,' said Clara, accepting Guy's arm and walking with him towards the entrance to the theatre. 'For instance, there is a rumour surfacing that some of our kind are stalking the human population and becoming rather adventurous around the West End. I have heard that there is apparently a group who can annihilate an entire houseful in seconds. All I can say, is that I would raise my hat to the individuals concerned regarding their expertise, but what prevents me from doing so, is the fact that we all know it is a complete waste of human life.' She sighed. 'There is a time and a place; it is in our nature to be secretive and they must ensure they are exceptionally careful. The last thing we want is some slayer hearing about it and crawling unfettered amidst the population.' She shuddered. 'Still, there is safety in numbers for our kind. We shall be quite safe tonight. The house is, as always, empty apart from myself. You are welcome to come back with me after we have eaten. I can ensure you have a perfect end to the evening.'

'That is an offer I cannot refuse, my love,' smiled Guy, 'but you have piqued my interest in this group you talk of.' He had a feeling that, if they were messy, violent kills, it was a group of relatively new and deeply crazed vampires that were storming the City. 'How many work within this pack, do they say?'

'That's the thing,' said Clara, looking up at him. 'Nobody knows. Opinion is divided – some people say it has to be a pack, and others suggest that there may just be one highly skilled and extraordinarily powerful vampire involved.' She smiled. 'There are never any witnesses.' She stopped suddenly and lifted her face to the evening breeze. It was a very faint smell, but she caught it; burning fabric, smouldering brickwork and seared flesh. 'Oh, I say. These idiots should invest in electricity - candle-lit events are simply too much of a fire risk, nowadays.'

Guy said nothing. He was remembering another ball, lit by candles, and a dark-haired vampire who had proved herself to be vicious and unrestrained. Was it just a co-incidence, he wondered? His instinct told him she was somehow involved. Not to worry, though. It wasn't his problem. He looked at Clara and smiled. 'Come on, then, you beautiful woman. The theatre, dinner and an evening at leisure awaits us.'

'How utterly perfect,' Clara said and smiled back at him.

Present Day

As usual, Drew greeted the next day with moans and groans and promises never to drink again. As usual, Lucas ignored him and was already packing his rucksack up for the day ahead.

'Time?' demanded Drew, his head buried under his pillow.

'Nine,' replied Lucas, pulling the zip closed. He slung the bag over his shoulder and turned to survey his friend. 'You missed breakfast.'

Drew murmured an expletive from the depths of the covers and forced his head out. 'So you didn't wake me. Thanks, mate,' he said.

Lucas shrugged. 'I tried,' he said. 'Anyway, the landlady says she's used to people like you. She's packed you a lunch up. If you're lucky, she might have a bit of toast left for you. I'm off.'

'Where you going?' asked Drew. 'I thought we were doing this one together?'

'That was the plan. But you slept in, mate. I've got to go. Got to be back for tea then up to the lime kilns.' He couldn't resist it. 'Places to go, people to see. If you know what I mean.'

'You what?' snapped Drew. He sat up in bed, wide awake. 'Who is it?'

'No-one you know,' said Lucas.

'The girl from last night?' pressed Drew 'The one from the bar?'

'The very same,' grinned Lucas, giving in. He'd thought about her last night in bed. What harm could it do? Really? All he had to do was meet up with her; spend a couple of hours with her and then say goodbye. They were leaving the Island the morning after. If it didn't work out, it didn't work out.

'So where are you off to then?' moaned Drew. 'You know - for this joint project of ours?'

'I'm going to the castle and the Gertrude Jekyll Garden,' announced Lucas heading towards the door. 'I'm picking up my lunch from the landlady. I won't be back until tea time, so have a good day. You know where I am if you want to meet up. It's not that big an island.' Drew muttered something unintelligible as Lucas closed the door on him. He headed down the narrow stairs and couldn't help but feel a little bit curious about the nooks and crannies

81

of the B&B. Little staircases and corridors seemed to branch off, and he couldn't quite get his bearings.

'Good morning,' said a fellow guest, standing in one of the corridors. Lucas looked up and paused. It was the tall, quiet man who had been in the lounge last night when he and Drew had rolled in sometime short of midnight. 'Did you sleep well?'

'Oh. Oh, yes. Thanks.' He felt the colour rise in his cheeks, suddenly remembering their laughter and lack of inhibitions. 'Ah no. I'm sorry, mate. Did we keep you awake?'

The man laughed and shook his head. 'Please don't concern yourself about that,' he said. 'I assume you had a good time?'

Lucas grinned. 'Yes. We did. Sorry again, mate. We'll be more quiet tonight. I won't be around for one thing. Well, not until later. Maybe.' The man raised his hands, palms up.

'You enjoy yourselves. I was young once. I remember the old hedonistic ways...' he laughed. 'They were good while they lasted.' He paused. 'I met some interesting people,' he said.

Lucas was intrigued. 'You're not that old!' he said. 'Sorry. That sounded wrong. You know what I mean though...' He decided to shut up before he dug himself in any deeper.

Fortunately, the man didn't seem bothered. He shrugged his shoulders. 'Ancient history,' he said, echoing Lucas' comments from last night about Laura. Something in Lucas' demeanour must have changed when he thought about it, because the man tilted his head to one side and stared at Lucas. 'Everything all right?' he asked.

'What? Oh yes. Yeah, fine thanks. Look, I'd best go. Sorry again about the noise,' replied Lucas heaving his bag onto his shoulder. 'We're all leaving tomorrow anyway. Just got to wait for the tide to turn and we'll be off I guess.'

'Not a problem,' said the man and stepped back, allowing him to pass.

Lucas had the distinct impression that the man watched him all the way down the stairs. It was a little un-nerving, actually. Almost like he was reading his mind. Lucas shook the thought away and found the landlady in the kitchen, her back towards the door.

'Excuse me, Mrs ummm... Mrs...errrr...' he said, embarrassed that he didn't know her name.

She turned from the bench where she was busy wrapping sandwiches in greaseproof paper and smiled at him. 'Christine is fine,' she said. 'We're not formal around here. I suppose you'll be wanting your lunch?' she reached behind the kettle and produced a paper bag which she held out to him. 'Everything you could need,' she said. 'I've put a bottle of water in there, but if you want a hot drink there's places you can get them on the island. We've plenty of tea-rooms.'

'I'd noticed,' said Lucas. 'Thanks again.'

'Be back for tea,' she said. 'It's crab salad. You should like it. My kids grew up with it. They can't stand it now.' She laughed. 'Best that they moved onto the mainland I suppose. Anyway, watch out for that tide, now. The tables tell you one thing, but with high winds and the like...' she shook her head. 'There's been too many accidents recently. And if I'm not mistaken, there's a storm blowing up.' Lucas thought about Cass and her promise to meet him at the lime kilns at five.

'So what's the safe crossing time?' he asked.

'You need to be off the shore by four, I would say, at the latest,' she said.

'What about the kilns? I was heading there later on,' he said.

Christine shook her head. 'I wouldn't want to be near them too close to high tide.' She shuddered. 'Nasty, dark place. It's all abandoned now, you know - nothing to see. If you can go there sooner, it's probably best. They fill up quite quickly when the tide comes in.'

'OK. Thanks. And thanks for this,' he said, raising the paper bag. 'I appreciate it.' He smiled and left the kitchen. He made up his mind to go to the kilns anyway, as he'd arranged. Cass was a local of sorts wasn't she? She should know whether it was safe at that time as well. And if they stayed on the cliffs and didn't try to clamber around the old, hollowed out tunnels, they would be fine: no problem.

***

The crab salad was out of this world. They all agreed it was definitely the best they'd ever tasted. The man from this morning was sitting alone, buried in the newspaper again. His salad lay partially eaten by his side and the landlady was fussing around him.

'Don't you like it?' she was saying. 'Can I get you anything else?'

'It's fine. I ate earlier. I made the mistake of filling up at lunch time,' laughed the man. 'It's no reflection on your cooking, honestly.'

'I could manage his leftovers,' muttered Drew, 'due to the fact I missed breakfast.' He glared at Lucas.

83

Lucas grinned, not taking offence. 'Well you've got tomorrow, mate,' he said. 'Make sure you fill up on breakfast then. It's a long way home.'

'Yeah, you're the one that'll be having the heavy night,' muttered Drew, reaching for the last bit of crusty, homemade bread slathered in farmhouse butter. 'I worked hard today, I deserve the crab salad.'

'Yeah, you worked hard when you eventually found me!' grinned Lucas. 'Anyway –a heavy night? Well, we'll have to see.' He looked at his watch. 'Oh, and it's time to leave. Right. I'm off. See you later.'

'Yeah. And I'll text you. Right in the middle of stuff,' threatened Drew.

'Pointless. No signal,' laughed Lucas. He stood up and slapped his friend on the back. 'Catch you later.'

It was grey and drizzly outside, the early December streets of London full of people and carriages rushing to their next appointment. Since Edward had come to the throne, the capital had been the centre of a dazzling social life – ideal for people to come and go as they wished, no questions asked. After all, if the King could do it, why couldn't they?

Genevieve preferred to shun society. She'd had enough of that at the Hall. The memory of that last ball was still with her, replayed over and over as she remembered Will and the summer house. Then she would recall her brother's face as she had borne down on him at the chapel and it would make her smile. She inhabited the world of two decades ago more and more often. For hours, she would sit on the floor and sing to herself, staring into space and living in the past. Cassandra was different. She was desperate to be amongst people, to see the operas and the plays, to visit the museums and the art galleries. Cassandra would often wander out into the city alone, wanting to experience as much as she could when Veva was otherwise occupied with thoughts of Will Hartley.

Cassandra felt that she had missed out on too much living. Always, foremost in her mind, was the memory of waking up, choking in agonising pain as venom flooded through her veins. She had opened her eyes and seen that girl there; the one who had killed Will. Veva. That was it. Cassandra had opened her mouth to scream and the girl had pounced on her, covering her mouth up with a cold, hard hand.

'Why? Why aren't you dead yet?' Veva kept saying. 'What have I done wrong?' With intense hatred in her eyes, the girl leaned over Cassandra. Cassandra saw her fangs and tried again to scream. Instinctively, she flung her arm upwards and the dark girl slammed across the room and hit the wall. Veva shrieked and ran at the bed again. Cassandra dragged herself upright and snarled. Veva had backed away and stared at her. Then she grabbed Cassandra by the throat.
'Did you even love Will?' she hissed. 'Because he's dead and you should be dead as well.'

'How dare you!' Cassandra had growled, ripping the girl's hands away. 'Will and I were to be married.'

'But did you love him?' repeated Veva. 'He was mine.' She narrowed her eyes. 'You took him away from me.'

'He wasn't yours,' replied Cassandra scathingly. 'They were never going to let him marry you. I knew all about you – all about the person he had disgraced at home – ha!' again, she deflected an angry swipe from Veva. Cassandra could feel the strength growing inside her and it felt good. 'I didn't want to come here until after the wedding, but he made me. I was supposed to think myself lucky that he had settled for me! How dare he?' Cassandra didn't know what had been in Will's mind, but she didn't like his attitude. Girls of her social standing didn't have much choice in the matter of marriage though. Orphaned at an early age, she had been brought up by a spinster aunt. The aunt had died, the families had made an 'arrangement' on the aunt's death bed and Cassandra had nowhere else to go.

Veva had continued staring at Cassandra. 'You must have known that you could never compete with me. He could never have loved you. Did you ever make love to him? I did. And I still love him, you know.'

'You put a bullet in his heart!' said Cassandra.

'And I would do it again!' snapped Veva. She pushed her face right up to Cassandra's. 'He was with you instead of me, wasn't he? So I would do it again. And again. And again. And I would kill anyone he was with. Over and over and over. But you – it didn't work. I tried. And I tried again tonight.' She reached out and pulled Cassandra from the bed, dragging her onto the floor. The girl fell into a heap, then, in one movement, launched herself at Veva.

Veva side-stepped out of the way and began to laugh. 'I can't believe that you won't die,' she said. 'I am so incompetent! Very well. It's quite clear that I shouldn't let you wander around like this. So, you have to come with me,' she said. 'And damn the lot of them.' Veva had raised her hand and cracked Cassandra across the face. The newborn vampire blacked out; she awoke several hours later huddled in a disused barn some miles away. Veva had dragged her out to the ruined chapel, telling her she couldn't leave her alone. Cassandra had seen Veva's brother, seen what vampires could be capable of, and quite quickly embraced her new life. She wouldn't have to answer to anyone anymore; well, apart from answering to Veva perhaps.

***

86

So the day that Cassandra wandered through the streets of London and found herself at the National Gallery in Trafalgar Square was not particularly unusual. She could sense a buzz about the place and decided to go inside. It had been a steep learning curve, but at least now she could move freely amongst people without wanting to rip their throats out. That pleasure, she reserved for night time and the people who nobody would miss, unless Veva had other plans. Cassandra tutted to herself. She would keep calling her Veva. It made it easier for them all round if she simply called her 'Jenny'. Veva was too unpredictable; she was getting worse. Sometimes, she seemed to relish being called Veva. She said it reminded her of Will, and she would drift off into her own world and begin humming that silly little tune which Cassandra now detested.

Cassandra knew the Impressionists had taken the art world by storm a few years ago. She and Veva had lived amongst them for a while; granted, the girls had been mostly un-noticed and routinely circled the very edge of the movement, but they were there. And it was during those years that Cassandra had discovered another love – that of the ballet. They had enjoyed that time. Veva had suddenly decided to take up art, and, as Veva had predicted all those years ago, Cassandra would slip away to haunt the opera and the theatre. She taught herself how to walk and move like a dancer and, in her head, she dreamed about a life devoted to that. Veva had dabbled with watercolours and pastels and drew the same thing over and over again; Will Hartley. Will in various attitudes: Will riding, Will laughing, Will lying dead on the floor... Her hands and mind worked ceaselessly, recreating him on canvas and staring for hours at the pictures. Living in Paris worked for a while, until the Bohemian lifestyle became too much for them. They found themselves drawn into it. Unable to restrain themselves, and with the body count mounting, they garnered suspicion and fled to England, where they lost themselves in London.

**

Cassandra filed into the National Gallery with the others, blending into the crowd with her perfect, s-shaped silhouette, white lace gown and wide-brimmed hat. The ribbon on her hat and the ribbon around her waist were almost the same azure-blue of her eyes. She also carried a parasol to shade her delicate skin, even though the rumours weren't true at all. Vampires did sleep and they didn't detest sunlight.

They simply found it too stimulating at times, thanks to their heightened senses.

'It's such a find!' said one woman leaving the Gallery, apparently with her husband. 'Imagine discovering all that work in an attic! I wonder who he was.' Cassandra was immediately alert.

'They think it dates from the true Impressionist period,' said another visitor, a young man this time – possibly a student. He was with a group of male friends. 'They said it's too old-fashioned to be post-Impressionism. The owner is set to make his fortune with that work.'

'Excuse me,' said Cassandra, placing her hand on the student's forearm, subtly restraining him. 'I'm terribly sorry, but I'm visiting the town today and I heard there was something exciting happening here?'

'Well, hello Miss!' blustered the boy as his friends sniggered behind him. 'Yes, it's definitely exciting. A new exhibition – it's called "*Found*". Some chap in Paris has discovered a collection of art in the attic rooms of his house, neatly hidden away behind fake walls! Incredible. They don't know who the artist was, but they say there is such passion in the portraiture that they wouldn't be surprised if it was a female, rather like Morisot. Allegedly, Cassat has denied it, but the Impressionist influences are stupendous. Truly amazing work.'

'I see. And what, pray tell, is the subject?' asked Cassandra lightly.

'That's just the thing – nobody knows. It's a man – it seems to be a series of paintings focussing on him. There is nothing to tell us who he is though. It's a major mystery. The owner is there today – he's very willing to speak to the public about it.'

'Thank you,' smiled Cassandra. 'I may just do that.' She released his arm and continued through the doorway, aware of his eyes following her. He was sweet and very young; rather harmless. She didn't mind him at all. She walked through the main vestibule and followed the stream of people. Most of the visitors were heading in one direction – she had a good idea where they were going.

Cassandra nodded as a curator held a door open for her and she stepped inside the exhibition room. Her eyes widened as she scanned the room and saw twenty five paintings of Will Hartley staring back at her.

***

Cassandra's emotions had long since stopped bothering her. Most of the time, she just switched them off and wasn't conscious of anything other than the task at hand. But this time, she was taken unawares. The hatred and anger bubbled up inside of her and she simply stood, staring at the paintings, unable to move. The memories of the last few days of her human existence bombarded her as she stood eye to eye with the man who had effectively ended her life.

'Are you quite well, my dear?' asked a voice. Cassandra dragged her gaze away from a picture which showed Will half-naked in what she assumed to be a summer house. His dark eyes looked back at her, mockingly. *Look at me*, he seemed to be saying. *Who wouldn't want to be with me? Are you envious?*

'It's very crowded in here,' she heard herself say. 'I did not expect the exhibition to be so popular.' She was looking at a man who was in perhaps his mid-forties. He had that arrogant look about him that she so despised in a man, yet she forced herself to smile at him. 'Are you the lucky gentleman who discovered these treasures?'

'I am indeed, my dear,' replied the man. He had a horrible, sweaty odour about his expensive clothing.
Cassandra compelled herself not to move away from him but smiled even wider. 'I would be very interested to hear the history behind them,' she said.

'There is nothing I would like more,' said the man, 'than to discuss it with you. It is very simple. I bought an old house in the middle of Paris and decided to do some renovations. Whilst my workmen were in the attics, they removed a false wall. All of these,' he swept his arm around the room, 'were hidden behind it. Along with some art equipment and a few unfinished sketches. Someone left in a hurry. I often wonder why they didn't take the paintings with them.'

'Did you perhaps do any research into previous occupants?' asked Cassandra. The man's body odour was distinctly unappealing and getting worse. She could smell his excitement at being so close to her.

'Oh, not really,' said the man dismissively. 'It was a very transient area of the city, very close to the Bohemian quarter. My sources think that it was a woman artist, but there is no trace of any female artist living there.'

'Well, Sir, I would imagine that she hid the portraits for a reason. Perhaps she never wanted them exhibited,' said Cassandra.

'Perhaps she didn't want people making money out of her.' She looked him in the eye and his gaze never wavered.

'Possession is nine-tenths of the law,' he replied smoothly. 'There are a few more I decided not to display. These ones here are the, shall we say, less *risqué* poses. If this is a success, I shall certainly bring the other ones out. They will cause ripples in the art world.' He laughed complacently. 'We live in interesting times. And I shall make quite a fortune out of this collection.'

Cassandra turned back to the pictures. She scanned the walls, suppressing an urge to drag her nails through each and every one of the portraits. She fought back the urge to drag her nails across the owner's throat as well. 'My sister would be very interested to see these,' she said. 'I must tell her to come along. She is quite interested in art. She knows a lot about that era of painting. I would not even be surprised if she could shed some light onto the subject matter. She has travelled quite extensively.'

'Is your sister anything like you?' the man asked.

'Very much so,' smiled Cassandra.

'Then I should be honoured to welcome both of you to my London residence. I have the rest of the collection there. You might like a rather more... *private* viewing?' The implication in his words was not lost on Cassandra.

She widened her eyes innocently. 'Really, Sir? How marvellous. When would be a suitable time to visit?'

'Tonight?' said the man. He picked up Cassandra's hand and kissed it. His mouth felt repulsively soft and wet on Cassandra's skin. 'This is my address.' He slipped a card into Cassandra's hand and she looked at it. It was one of the better streets in London – in Mayfair, no less. Albemarle Street.

The man poked the card with a podgy forefinger. 'I am renting at the moment, but I do intend to buy when I sell some of the artwork,' he said. 'May I suggest seven p.m.?'

'We shall look forward to it, Mr...?'

'Worthing. Mr Francis Worthing.'

'Wonderful.' Cassandra curtsied slightly. 'Until later. *Adieu*, Mr Worthing.'

The man laughed. 'You speak French!' he said.

'We lived there for a while,' smiled Cassandra. 'As I said, we have travelled extensively.' She turned her back on him, careful not to look at any more of Veva's paintings. *Interesting times*, he had said. Well. Tonight would be *very* interesting.

***

'Tell me again why we need to be here?' asked Veva. A flutter of confusion passed across her face. Cassandra had noticed these little episodes were becoming more frequent.

'This gentleman has found something and I think you might want to see it,' Cassandra replied. 'You like art, don't you? He has some paintings you might like. You might have an idea what to do with them. He wants to display them but I don't think that's the right thing to do. It needs an expert opinion.'

'I love art,' smiled Veva. 'Paris was wonderful, wasn't it? We should go back. You could dance, if you wanted to.'

'Perhaps,' said Cassandra. 'Look, this must be his house here.' They had walked, keeping to the dark streets as they always did now when they went out at night. They had learned in Paris, that the less people who saw them, the less chance there was of discovery.

'I still don't understand why you think I need to be here,' said Veva. 'You've worked well all these years. I'm sure you are more than capable of making the decision yourself.' Cassandra knew exactly what she meant by "decision".

'It's just that you need to see him as well. To be honest, I think it's rather more important that you see the paintings. I can deal with him.'

Veva shrugged her shoulders. 'As you wish,' she said.

Cassandra reached up and knocked on the door. A gentleman who wasn't Mr Francis Worthing opened it.

'Ah. You must be the guests,' he said.

Cassandra frowned. 'I'm sorry, do we know you?' she asked. 'We came to see Mr Worthing. Or, more exactly, we came to see his newly-acquired paintings.'

'Well, Mr Worthing and I come as a package,' smiled the man. 'As I believe you and your sister do.' He stepped to one side and beckoned them in. Cassandra glided past him, and Veva followed, staring at him oddly. The girls waited in the reception area until the man shut the door and he took them upstairs.

'We will be entertaining you up here,' he said. 'Mr Worthing has given the staff the night off.'

'How fortunate for them,' murmured Veva. Cassandra half-smiled. She understood exactly what she meant. Good. She only

91

hoped her own intentions weren't as noticeable. The man pushed open the door and Mr Francis Worthing sat, his bulk resplendent in a smoking jacket, smiling at the girls.

'Ahh, you found us,' he said. 'Excellent. A drink?'

'No, thank you,' replied Cassandra. 'We did come to, umm, see the paintings? As you recall?'

'Yes. I do recall,' said Mr Worthing. 'But before that, please, let me introduce my friend. Clarence Burgess Esq.'

Veva had walked off, apparently tired of the banal conversation and she was staring out of the window at the street below. 'You haven't allowed us to introduce ourselves,' Veva said. 'That's rather impolite, is it not?' She turned and smiled sweetly at the gentlemen. 'Or do our names not interest you?'

'Well I wouldn't say that,' said Worthing.

'Hmm,' said Veva.

Cassandra heard her quietly begin to hum and she bowed her head to hide a smile. 'Not yet, darling,' she murmured, lowering her voice.

'Please, sit down, Miss...err. Miss... and Miss...ummm.' Worthing faltered.

Veva laughed. 'Please don't concern yourself,' she said. She sat down on the chaise longue and looked at Clarence Burgess Esq. 'Are you the gentleman who likes art?' she asked. She lay back on the chair and tilted her head to the side. She had left her hair loose tonight and pinned an artificial rose into the side. Cassandra, on the other hand, had swept her hair up into a complicated chignon. Both men studied Veva and Cassandra felt the old jealousy prick her. It was never her, was it? Much as she hated these men and others like them, for once, just *once*, she would like to be the centre of attention. Veva eclipsed her though. She always had done. As far back as Will Hartley.

'Mr Worthing is the art lover,' Cassandra interjected. 'He made a very exciting discovery. Didn't you, Mr Worthing?' She made a point of sitting next to Veva, so the men would have to notice her too.

'Oh. Yes, I did,' Mr Worthing replied. He heaved himself out of his seat and moved over to the doorway. He picked up a scrapbook and brought it over to the girls. 'This is my house in Paris,' he said. 'The refurbishment is almost complete. Work stopped when we made the discoveries.' Veva cast a glance at Cassandra, a question

92

in her eyes. She reached out and took the book from Mr Worthing and bent her head over it.

The men wouldn't have noticed, but Cassandra did; Veva stiffened and her fingers grasped the edge of the book. 'You say you made some discoveries?' she said, her voice tight. 'Where, may I ask, did you find them? And, more importantly, what were they?' She looked up and Cassandra felt a little thrill when she saw the shutters half come down in her eyes.

'Did your sister not tell you?' asked Mr Worthing? 'It is an exhibition that is taking London by storm. I call it "Found".' He smiled complacently. 'Clever, yes? A pile of canvasses, clearly created by a genius, and all discovered by accident. The art world is frantic.'

'It was my idea,' said Burgess. 'Francis is my business partner. We have consolidated some assets with this little lot. I have had contracts drawn up to ensure that I get my commission from any works sold...'

'Sold?' snapped Veva. 'What's to be sold?'

'Why, the paintings, of course!' said Cassandra. 'Mr Worthing only has a few on display. The rest are here, I presume. That's what we are here to see, darling. You might recognise the artist...or the subject.'

Veva glared at Cassandra. 'Truthfully?' she said.

Cassandra looked at her innocently. 'Yes. Truthfully.' She turned to Mr Worthing. 'I think it's time to see the pictures now, before we move onto anything else?' There was a promise in her voice.

'This way, my dear,' said Mr Worthing. 'I have them in this room, just through here.' He pushed open another door and stood back. 'Enjoy. My particular favourite is...' he stumbled as Veva rushed past him. 'Steady on girl! No need to move so fast. There's a fortune in there! Be careful, won't you?'

Veva pulled up short in the middle of the room and stood, rooted to the spot. '*Will*,' she said. 'My work...' She turned around and looked at Cassandra who had followed her in. 'It's Will.' The madness and desperation were there, just behind the perfect features.

'Oh?' said Cassandra. She looked around, forcing herself to meet his eyes on the paintings. They were skilfully done; each stroke conveyed passion and desire. Will stared out at the viewer, inviting them into his life. How she wished she could eradicate him forever! How she had dwelt on him over the years and how she hated him.

'So it is,' Cassandra said. 'Oh look. I remember that one very well.' She took Veva firmly by the shoulders and turned her around. Facing her was a huge canvas of Will lying on the drawing room floor. Veva had done something to the picture which made him appear to be lying there, just waiting for a woman to discover him *in flagrante*, rather than make him look as if he had just been murdered. 'Actually, that one's quite good as well.' She pulled Veva around and made her look at another one; a smaller canvas, again of his face, clearly after he had been shot and killed. But again, unless you had been there, he simply looked sensual. 'I say, there are quite a few like this, aren't there? He looks rather...dead. Who could have done that to him? Oh yes. You did, didn't you?'

That was enough to make her snap. Veva threw Cassandra's hands off her shoulders and flew at her. The two men, terrified, turned and tried to run out of the room. Veva caught the movement out of the corner of her eye and she whipped around. It only took an instant and they both lay dead. She turned back to Cassandra and went for her again. Cassandra laughed and side-stepped her, the way Veva had avoided Cassandra's attack so long ago. 'Yes, darling. It was all your own work, wasn't it? All of this. Wasn't it? Veva.'

Veva faltered and the shutters went down completely. Cassandra smiled to herself. She had created a perfect storm; she had forced Veva to face a reality she had long since rejected and placed her, quite deliberately, in that room full of memories. The icing on the cake, as they said, was the simple addition of her name. *Et, voila*.

'My work?' Veva said. She stared at Cassandra as if suddenly she didn't know who she was or anything about what had just happened. 'I did it? What did I do?' She shook her head. 'No. That was Veva. That was an awfully long time ago.' That, Cassandra realised, was the moment it had happened; the moment Veva's mind finally shattered. Veva sat down in the middle of the floor, facing the huge canvas depicting Will's death. She automatically reached up and pulled the rose out of her hair, shredding it to pieces on the floor. Cassandra waited for a moment, and sat down carefully next to her. They both surveyed the painting. Veva had disappeared into a world even darker than the one she had existed in for almost twenty years.

'Please stop that annoying humming, darling,' said Cassandra eventually. 'I'm sorry. Actually. No, I'm not sorry. I'm sorry that I met you. And I'm sorry that I met Will. I'm sorry that my life choices were taken away from me; although I don't exactly dislike my life.' She paused, thoughtfully. She turned to Veva and put her arm around her unresisting shoulders. 'It's the only way I could destroy you, darling,' said Cassandra, as if they were having a perfectly normal conversation. 'I couldn't get you any other way. This way, we can be stronger. And maybe I'll be able to make some decisions now, hmm?' She sighed, studying Veva's perfect face and dark eyes. 'I can't stop men preferring you, though can I?' she leaned over and kissed her on the forehead. Veva continued shredding the rose until there was nothing left of it. Then she moved on to the ruffles on her skirts. Cassandra took hold of her hand and stilled it. She looked across at the bodies of the two men who had inadvertently helped her. It was a shame. That was a kill she would have enjoyed. 'We will be able to make this work to our advantage,' she said thoughtfully. 'Oh, I suppose you'll come out of this eventually. When you do, I'll call you Jenny. I promise.'

To the untutored eye, the dark-haired girl could easily have passed for a beautiful, slightly unbalanced young lady. It would be harder, though, to ignore the smears of blood all over her white dress and all around her perfect mouth. Cassandra knew, however, that there were certain dangers beneath the surface. It would take her a little while to work out how to manage the situation, but she had all the time in the world.

Present Day

Christine, the landlady, had been right. There was definitely a storm brewing. The clouds were low and glowering over the outline of the Priory. Even from here, Lucas was convinced he could hear the swell of the North Sea as it broke over the sandbanks and covered the beach. He'd ventured onto the rocks near the castle earlier and almost fell flat on his face as he stepped on the slimy, green seaweed that covered everything. Now, he could feel drops of rain starting to fall, hitting him on the face as the wind carried them off the coast. He swore under his breath. Bloody Godforsaken place that it was...then he quickly corrected himself. How could it be Godforsaken when there was that huge Priory here? Still. It wasn't pleasant and he wouldn't have fancied being a monk all those centuries ago. He was sure that on a sunny, dry day it was stunning. He'd been amazed at the upturned fishing boats along the shore; all brightly coloured with piles of orange lobster pots jumbled around them. He'd spoken to a couple of the locals as they sat mending nets, and visited the castle along with most of the tourists on the Island. He'd had his lunch in the scrubby little square that was the Gertrude Jekyll Garden and wished there were a few more flowers in bloom. He was sure it was a little oasis on the Island for the nature lovers. Drew had eventually found him there and they'd worked companionably all afternoon. He'd deflected Drew's probing questions about the girls; he had the distinct impression that Drew quite liked Jenny. If he was honest, he liked her too. He shook the thought away. It was Cass he had arranged to meet tonight. He felt a bit disloyal, thinking about her sister like that. And to be fair, Jenny would probably be quite high maintenance.

He walked on towards the lime kilns and shivered as the wind blew harder. Definitely a storm coming. He could see the stone arches across the bay and a figure standing on top of them. It lifted its arms up and waved at him, then turned and ran down the grassy track between the rocks. He increased his pace and put his head down into the wind, pushing onwards. Those kilns were enormous. If he stood still long enough, he was sure he could imagine the noise of the fires and the smell of the burning lime, coupled with the shouts of the workers. It must have been a very different picture a century and a half ago.

'Lucas! Oh thank *goodness* you're here!' The figure bore down on him and he started. It was Jenny. She looked terrified; her eyes were huge in her white face, her hair even more dishevelled than before. She had somehow pulled it around into a side ponytail, caught with an elastic band beside her chin and tendrils escaped everywhere. She flung herself into his arms and he stood, feeling the coldness of her body. She must have been there ages. She was wearing a short sleeved lacy top and a little pleated skirt above thick black tights. She wasn't wearing any shoes.

'You're freezing!' he said. 'What's up?'

'It's Cass,' she said. 'She didn't come home. She went over onto the mainland earlier. She walked, I told her not to. She rang me from the other side – there's a phone box, did you see it?' Lucas shook his head – he couldn't recall seeing one, but then he wasn't looking for one when they had crossed the causeway. 'She rang and said she was heading over the causeway. She thought she had plenty of time. I think she's drowned, Lucas! I think she's dead!'

'Hold on, hold on!' he said. His heart started pounding. This was all he needed. 'She's not dead. She won't be dead. She's sensible.'

Jenny began to sob. 'I'm worried, Lucas. I'm so worried. I knew she was meeting you here. I hurried over. I thought if she was running late, she'd have come straight here. She hates letting people down...'

Lucas didn't speak. He held Jenny close and stroked her hair. 'It's OK, it's OK,' he whispered.

Jenny lifted her tear-stained face up to his. 'I like you Lucas. I really do. But Cass saw you first. You're a nice person; a good person. In some ways I want her dead as I can have you then...but that's a really bad thing to think, isn't it?' She stared up at him. 'Isn't it? You're shocked aren't you? I'm a horrible person. My family always thought I was a horrible person.' Then suddenly she laughed. 'They're all dead too. That's awful, isn't it? It's just me and Cass now, and I'm worrying that she's going to leave me, but I'm telling you I want her out of the way. God!' She flung herself away from Lucas and sort of concertinaed onto the ground. She sat on the wet grass, her hair plastered across her face and stared out to sea. 'Can you help me, Lucas? I need help.'

'I – I don't know what to say...' he began.

Jenny laughed again. Then it turned into another heaving sob. 'Sit down, Lucas. Sit down next to me. Can you think what we can do? I can't leave her out there alone. Maybe she's in the refuge hut? Do you think she's in the refuge hut, Lucas? Can we find out?'

Lucas followed her gaze, seeing the greyish-white hut that stood proud of the waves. 'There's a light on inside the hut!' he said suddenly. 'Look!'

Jenny sprang to her feet and leaned forward, as if she could get a better view of the hut. 'There is! Oh –Lucas. If it flashes out her name in Morse code, it's her!'

'What?' asked Lucas, staring at her.

'It was my idea.' Jenny giggled. 'Didn't Cass tell you I was creative? I thought it was a really good idea. It's our signal to each other.' Her face crumpled again. 'You don't like it, do you? You think I'm stupid.'

'No, you're not stupid. That's actually really clever,' he said.

Jenny threw herself back into his arms and took his face between her hands. 'I knew I liked you. I knew it. Kiss me, Lucas. Please. Cass will never know... she always gets the boys. I never do. If you kiss me, it will make me so happy.' Lucas couldn't help himself. He leaned forward and covered her hands with his. He closed his eyes and kissed her. Jenny pulled away first. Lucas opened his eyes and saw a smile playing about her lips. 'Thank you, Lucas. We'll not tell her. It can be our secret.' She pushed him away gently and turned back to face the refuge hut. 'It will flash any second...now,' she stated: it was as if, Lucas thought with a stab of annoyance, the kiss hadn't actually meant anything to her at all.

Sure enough, he saw the lights waver in the refuge hut. They flashed on and off. He couldn't make what they were supposed to be doing, but Jenny started jumping up and down.

'That's a C. That's an A...an S...another S...it's her! Lucas, it's her! Can you go and get her? Please? If you don't I will. That's my rowing boat there – I'm going for her...' Jenny started scrambling down the slippery grass and heading towards the boat that was being tossed around on the waves. 'She'll be scared on her own,' she shouted back over her shoulder, pausing on the slope, silhouetted against the sea. Lucas caught his breath; she was the most stunning creature he'd ever seen.

'No! No, Jenny,' he shouted, 'you can't go out in this. I'll go. You go home, go and wait there for her. Do you need to let the coastguard know or something?'

Jenny shook her head. 'I don't think so,' she said. She frowned a little, confused. 'Do I?'

Lucas slid down the hill towards her. He grabbed hold of her arm and tried to tug her away from the shore. 'I'm going Jenny. I'll see you later.'

'Will you telephone me from the hut?' she asked.

'How can I? There's no signal.'

'Didn't you bring a telephone?' she asked, opening her eyes wide. She sat down again. 'That's good. I'll just wait here.'

Exasperated, Lucas pulled her to her feet. 'No. Go home,' he said.

She clung onto him and kissed him again. 'I will see you soon, Lucas,' she smiled.

Lucas disengaged himself and waded over to the boat. He climbed into the boat and settled himself best he could. The North Sea had sloshed into his trainers and soaked through his jeans: and the seats on the boat were soaking too. He looked back at the shore and saw Jenny. Exasperating though she was, she was still stunning. He just couldn't deal with all these conflicting signals. Jenny raised her hand to her lips and blew another kiss. Then she pulled the band out of her hair, wound it around her wrist and sat down on the ground again. She didn't even seem to be that cold. It was getting dark now and the moon was breaking through the clouds. Lucas began to row.

The place to be in London during the so-called 'swinging sixties' was either Carnaby Street or the King's Road in Chelsea. The area was the hub of sixties glamour and anyone who was anyone in the world of fashion design had a presence there. There were some marvellous shops, Clara had told Guy. The theatre was boring now; next time he visited, he had to take her shopping. Guy had wanted to know what he would gain out of it. Beatniks and bohemia were not his pleasures, he had told her. Clara had laughed and said 'ah': but *she* was his pleasure. Guy had to agree. So it was that he found himself absorbed in the hustle and bustle of London yet again. Clara greeted him wearing a tiny mini-skirt and knee length white boots; but Guy, although appreciative of her charms, was still unsure of modern day fashions: a by-product of the time when women wore long skirts and bustles. Clara told him he needed to understand the concept of Biba and Mary Quant.

'The wonderful thing about our lives is that we can evolve as we need to,' Clara said. She hung onto his arm as they strolled down Carnaby Street looking in the windows of the boutiques they passed. Clara lived in a flat now, a three bedroomed affair, converted from an old Victorian house in the Swiss Cottage area of Hampstead in North London. It was the perfect compromise. She still lived in a style of house dear to her heart, but in a flat, one found there was a very fluid population in the building - nobody wondered why she never aged and what her story was. It suited her. Guy remained non-plussed with the fashion revolution. He was simply there as Clara's companion, staying at her home and sharing her bed, but even he realised that it wasn't as easy to haunt the East End and feed these days. There was, of course, the gang culture. If people disappeared at random, one of the gangs would get the blame – but it wasn't ideal. You would always have the runaways, though – the ones who left their homes to 'find themselves' within the LSD and cannabis induced haze of the London Scene.

'Look at this!' Clara exclaimed, drawing to a halt outside a designer boutique. She wore huge, black sunglasses and pushed them up onto her head. Her eyes were just as green as ever, the red around the irises not as noticeable today. She pointed at a silver necklace in the window, showing a tiny dagger on a silver chain. The detail was precise and she pressed her hands against the window. 'Oh my, now that is rather special,' she said.

Guy looked at it without much interest. 'It's simply a necklace,' he said shrugging.

'Look at the craftsmanship,' she said. 'I wonder if it's vintage?' Then she laughed. 'Wouldn't that be the very thing - perhaps that there is the stuff of vampire legend. Now wouldn't that just spoil our folklore? Imagine if that was the replica dagger the Slayer had created.'

'Replica dagger?' repeated Guy. He looked at the necklace more closely.

'Yes,' said Clara. 'It was created sometime before you were re-born. Haven't I told you? How lax of me.' She pouted. 'And I thought I had taught you so well. You're far more civilised than many of us. I shall take credit for that at least.'

'You may certainly take credit for that, but you have told me nothing about a dagger,' said Guy. He concentrated on steadying his voice. He knew that, wrapped in a towel, in a drawer at his country estate was the dagger he had taken the first night of his new life. He had taken it, he remembered, for protection. He had carried it with him for a short while until he became more confident about his new abilities. He didn't need it now and he certainly didn't need protection.

'Oh dear! I am sorry. It's quite exciting, really. There is a legend which suggests a silver dagger was created to kill vampires and then it was subsequently lost in the Crusades. So, we were all safe for several centuries. Then, about one hundred years ago, evidence appeared which seemed to suggest that a jeweller in Clerkenwell had been commissioned to make a replica of the dagger. Several of our kind made a pact to locate it, and one young female never returned from her quest. Legend has it, that she had discovered the dagger and the owner. The dagger went missing, but everyone knew that someone was using it – certain vampires simply disappeared and it was all just too coincidental. The last anyone heard, was a rumour that some stupid half-witted girl in the slums had lost it.' Clara pulled a face. 'They get too confident, you see, these new ones. They think they are invincible and become careless. Nobody ever managed to trace the girl who had lost it – she probably didn't even know what it was. Or that she had even lost it!'

Guy nodded. 'That makes a lot of sense,' he said carefully.

'Oh, it gets better!' laughed Clara. She replaced the sunglasses on her face. 'The so-called slayer blessed it with Holy Water from a Priory in Lindisfarne in Northumberland and they say he buried a phial of it up there to keep it safe.' She shuddered. 'The thought of even setting foot in a place like that repulses me. I hope it is just a legend and it stays buried, if indeed it is true.'

'I suppose that one would need to acquire the dagger and the Holy Water,' said Guy lightly, 'in order to ensure our type were safe.'

'Yes, I suppose that would be a plan,' smiled Clara, 'if indeed it were all true. In the meantime, I think I shall purchase this little bagatelle. It is rather sweet and an excellent talking point.' She reached up and kissed him. 'I am so sorry, darling, I thought I had taught my little protégé everything he needed to know.'

Guy smiled. 'You are my dearest friend, Clara,' he said. He bowed slightly to her and she laughed.

'You are still so old-fashioned,' she said. 'Come inside with me.'

'I don't think so,' he said. 'I have some business to attend to. I will find a telephone and call my contacts to see what is happening. There were some issues I needed resolving at home.'

Clara nodded. 'Of course, darling,' she said. 'If there are any...issues...I can help you resolve, do let me know.' She leaned in towards him and whispered in his ear. 'I do love a good kill.'

'You are my first recourse to action,' he whispered back. 'I will return shortly, I promise.' She kissed him again and pushed the door open to the boutique, disappearing inside. Guy walked a little way along the road and ducked up a side street in case she came out and looked for him. He had no calls to make, of course, no issues at home to resolve; he just needed an excuse to leave London as soon as possible. Then he would go back to the estate, collect the dagger and travel up north. This way, if it all worked to plan, Sir Guy Montgomery would be the invincible one.

'*Do you wanna know a secret...*' The Beatles thrummed out of the radio and Christine lay back on the grass, taking a long drag from a cigarette.

'It's nice here, isn't it?' she asked, looking sidelong at the young man lounging beside her. It was his vehicle. One of those VW bus things that were so popular. The van had a sort of bed in it that converted from a seat. The blankets were pretty messed up now, that was why they had come outside into the salty air, catching some welcome daylight before the sun dropped into the North Sea in a great, big fiery orange ball.

'Yes. It is very nice,' he agreed. He stretched his long legs out in front of him and clasped his hands behind his head. 'I haven't seen much of the Island today. Would you be so kind as to take me for a tour? Later on, maybe, when it's darker. And there are fewer people about.'

'When the tide turns, you mean?' asked Christine.

'I mean exactly that. I hear there is a very pleasant Priory here.'

'Oh, that,' said Christine, stubbing the cigarette out on the ground next to her. 'Yes, I suppose. Not much to see though. Just some old ruins.'

'Sometimes old ruins are very exciting,' said her companion.

'Old ruins? You are a bit strange!' said Christine. 'The pub is better. I know the barmaid. Not hard – I know bloody everyone on this island,' she laughed at her own joke. 'What I mean,' she continued, rolling onto her side and trailing her forefinger down his chest, 'is that I can get a bottle of wine from her. Cheap, like. Or maybe two bottles. Or beer. Would you like beer? Then we can take it down the beach and light a fire. Or maybe just take it in your van. We can drink it...and just enjoy ourselves. You know?' At twenty, Christine was just on the brink of womanhood. She knew she would have to settle down soon. Probably end up marrying one of the fishermen on the island. Probably spend the rest of her days here, raising kids and cooking meals and pandering to tourists. Her mam and dad owned a B&B. She'd probably inherit that. Her older brother had buggered off down south and her little sister was determined to follow him as soon as she finished school. Christine had always been the sensible one; the one they expected to stay here. So this was her little rebellion. Well, one of her little rebellions. She liked the tourists that came to the Island. She always gave them a warm welcome – well, the good looking blokes at least. She looked at the chap she was with tonight. He was something else. Posh, like. Proper posh - like London posh... For Christ's sake, he called himself Montgomery! How bloody posh was that?

'Thank you,' smiled Montgomery. 'I think I'll pass on the beer and the wine this time. Not really my thing. But I would love for you to take me to the Priory - only if you want to. I have to leave tomorrow, so if you won't accompany me, I'm afraid I'll just have to go myself. Just point me in the right direction and I'll be fine.'

Christine scowled. That was the worst of these tourists, she thought. They never stayed very long. This one was really nice as well. A gentleman. She sighed. The Priory it was, then. If only so she got to spend a wee bit longer with him. She'd get a couple of bottles anyway – bring them to his van with a few sausages and a loaf of her mam's bread. They could eat and drink later, after the bloody Priory. 'OK,' she said. 'I'll come over later. About nine-ish? I have to help with the dinners, but we'll be done by then.' She pulled a face. 'It's crab again anyway. You'd think they'd get sick of it.'

'Will the tide have turned by nine?' Montgomery asked. He rolled onto his side, smiling lazily at her. Christine's heart did a little flip. Now, how could she resist that smile? His hand caught hers and he lifted it to his mouth. He gave it a little kiss and pulled her towards him. 'You won't tell anyone where you're taking me, will you?' he asked.

'God, no!' stuttered Christine. Her heart was beating crazily. This bloke knew exactly which buttons to press. 'Whatever you want to do, that's fine. I'll do it...whoops,' she giggled. 'That sounded bad didn't it?'

'Not at all,' murmured Montgomery, peppering her hand and the inside of her wrist with tiny kisses.

'Oh Lord!' said Christine. Her arm was tingling like buggery. It was all she could do not to leap on him there and then; she felt the colour rise in her cheeks.

'Will you remember me when you leave here?' breathed Christine. She edged closer to him and got to her knees. She planted herself in front of him and looked down at him.

'I'm sure I will remember you,' he said. 'Come on, let's make sure I do.' He eased himself up and pulled her to her feet. He stood back to let her in the VW and followed her inside it; then he slid the door to and it closed with a soft click.

**

Christine snuck out of the B&B at quarter to nine. She nipped across the road to the pub and, sure enough, her friend slipped her a couple of bottles of wine.

'Enjoy yourself,' winked Ellen. 'Don't need me to tell you that, though, do you? If you can't be good, be careful and all that.'

Christine rolled her eyes theatrically. 'Cheers Ellen. Like you wouldn't do the same!' she said.

'I so would,' laughed Ellen, 'if I could get a bloody night off!'

'I'll be thinking of you,' said Christine. She waved the bottles at her friend. 'While I'm drinking these.'

'Get out!' cried Ellen, giving her a gentle push. 'I'll see you tomorrow.' Christine laughed and hurried out of the pub, padding down the lane towards the field where Montgomery was. The tide had turned and the Island was cut off from everything now. She could just make out Montgomery's van, and saw him pacing in front of it. She sped up and ran the last few yards, stumbling on the grassy tussocks in the field. He turned sharply as she approached him and he stood waiting for her.

'Hello!' she gasped a little breathlessly. 'I've brought some wine after all. Oh and some sausages. Just thought you might be hungry after the walk...'

The man sighed. 'I told you not to bother,' he said. 'I won't be having any of it.'

'Oh,' Christine said, deflated. 'I thought...'

'Never mind,' he said. 'Put them in the van.' He slid the door open and Christine laid the bottles down next to the packet of sausages just inside the door. She straightened up.

'Is everything all right?' she asked as he slammed the door shut. The sound echoed around the field.

'It's not an issue,' he said. 'I'm sorry. I'm just a little on edge, that's all. You haven't told anyone where we are going, have you?'

She shook her head. 'No,' she said, 'no, I haven't.' She heard him take a deep breath and saw him smile in the dusk.

'Good. I want this to be special. A private moment for us. After all, it's possibly our last night together.'

105

'Oh *don't!*' she whined. 'I don't want to think about tomorrow!'

'You don't have to,' he said. 'Come with me. Let's forget our little disagreement and have a nice wander to the Priory.'

Christine relaxed a little and took the arm he held out to her. She allowed him to lead him towards the Priory.
Once, he asked if they could stay off the main road. 'I don't want anyone spoiling our last night,' he told her. 'Is it possible to go a different way?'

'Oh – well, yes. We can take a shortcut, if you like,' said Christine. It was rather sweet of him to squeeze her hand so tightly and whisper, '*thank you my darling,*' when they turned off onto a tiny lane. She slowed the pace right down. Maybe he wanted some privacy with her? She felt herself blushing in the cool night air at the thought and was pleased that it was too dark for him to see her properly.

Nevertheless, he laughed softly. 'What is it?' he asked. 'I can tell you're blushing.' He brought his lips close to her cheek and kissed her softly.

'Oh Lord,' she muttered. It was all she could do to stop herself dragging him off into the bushes.

He laughed at her again and pulled away. 'Are we far, my darling?' he asked.

'No, it's just around the corner. See? You can just make out the arch through those trees.'

Montgomery exhaled. 'At last,' he said. They rounded the corner and stopped outside the Priory. 'I'm going in,' he said, leaving go of her arm. 'It's something I just have to do on my own. Please forgive me. I shall collect you in a few moments...'

'Ah. You're doing a pilgrimage thing,' said Christine. She wrinkled her nose up. She was used to tourists coming here and doing that sort of thing. Last year, though, a couple of people had been drowned – stupid people who didn't take notice of the tide tables. Come to think of it, last year hadn't been very good at all. Ellen's brother had headed down south for the work, like Christine's brother. He'd been nice, had Frank. He'd more or less promised Christine he'd marry her, but he had a new life now and didn't keep in touch with anybody much.

'A pilgrimage?' asked Montgomery, interrupting her thoughts. 'Well, I suppose you could say that. I shan't be long.' He turned to Christine and inclined his head. 'Thank you.' He melted away into the Priory ruins and Christine sat down on a rock to wait for him.

***

Christine didn't know how long she had been there, but she was starting to get pretty cold. She stood up on her tiptoes to see if she could see any movement in the Priory ruins. Ridiculous, really; it was far too dark now to see anything.

'Sod this,' she said out loud, and began to pick her way through the fallen stones at the edge of the Priory. It was eerie in the ruins at night. The arch loomed over everything, blacker even than the sky. Christine shivered. 'Hello?' she called out. Her voice wavered in the darkness. There was a strange sense of...something...at the Priory. She didn't quite know what it was. It just felt different. 'Montgomery?' she tried. His name sounded odd. She realised it was the first time she had actually used it. It was dead posh and felt wrong somehow. She called again, trying to make her voice stronger. 'Montgomery? Are you there? I'm sorry – I know you might be pilgrimage-ing or whatever it is, but it's been ages. You said you wouldn't be long?' Nothing. She made her way through the nave to the eastern end and her foot slipped off a paving slab. 'Ouch!' she cried. She stood for a moment rubbing her ankle; the silence felt suffocating. 'Hello?'

Then she saw him. He was hunched up by the wall, sitting with his arms wrapped around his legs and staring at the ground.

'Thank God! Are you all right?' she asked, kneeling down. She put her hand on his shoulder and he flinched.

'Yes. You're right. Thank God,' he said. He put his hand up and grabbed Christine's. She jumped. His grasp was freezing cold and so strong it hurt. 'Thank God for what He has shown me tonight. I have to change things. I have to make them better. I shouldn't have done it to her.' he stared at Christine, as if seeing her properly for the first time. 'At least I didn't hurt you. I shouldn't have done it to her, though, it was wrong. I see that now. She was wild. She's still wild. God help me. What have I done?' He took his hand away from hers and covered his face with both hands.

'Bloody Hell,' said Christine. She started to rub his back, like she used to do with her little sister when she was upset. 'Are you OK?' Her voice tailed off. It felt weird comforting him. She hardly knew him. She took her hand away from his back.

The man moved his hands from his face and stared into the distance. 'She's going to come back, you know. I was meant to come here and find this. He's helped me,' said Montgomery. Christine thought he meant God had helped him, but then she realised that Montgomery was pointing at something she couldn't quite see. He seemed to be focussed on a patch of the wall by the *piscina*; there seemed to be some sort of dark shadow standing there. Christine blinked and whatever it was disappeared.

'I think we should go,' she said. 'It's a bit strange in here tonight. I don't like it much.' She looked over her shoulder, as if she were expecting a procession of monks to walk down the nave. 'No. I don't like it. Are you coming?'

The man shook his head. 'No. Not just yet. I'll come when I'm ready.' He picked something off the ground and turned it in his hands. It was difficult to see, but Christine thought it was a small bottle. 'I have to be careful. I can't let this break. It will destroy me. I need to keep it safe. I can't take the chance.'

Oh Lord, it's the drink! She thought. Her dad had told her about people who couldn't handle it. They came to the Island and drank the mead and wondered why it sent them crazy. It was powerful stuff, that mead. Montgomery was obviously the same. He'd come here, had a bit too much in the Priory there, and was regretting it. No wonder he hadn't wanted the wine she'd brought. He must have been trying to stay off it, he'd failed and now he wasn't making a lot of sense.

'Um. Well, look, I'll tell you what,' said Christine. 'I'll head back to your van and wait for you there shall I?' Then she thought again. If he was as mad as this, what would he be like when he'd had the rest of that mead? People like that couldn't resist the drink, could they? 'No. Actually I won't. I'll go home, and if you're still here tomorrow, I'll come and see you, yes? Let you sleep it off...I mean, let you have some rest.'

'I intend staying here a while longer,' said Montgomery. 'There are a lot of things I need to atone for. I think that is the best solution. Perhaps I will see you tomorrow. Goodbye, Christine. Thank you for bringing me here.'

'Um– that's fine. No problem,' she said. 'I'll see you tomorrow. 'Bye, then.' She hovered uncertainly for a moment, then realised she wasn't going to get anything else out of him. She turned and ran back through the nave, back out of the Priory and onto the lane. She looked around her. There was definitely a weird feeling about this place tonight and too many things she didn't fully understand. She remembered the image of the dark shadow by the *piscina* and decided to go back home on the road, rather than down the back lanes. She had never felt so pleased to be heading home. Before too long, she could see the lights of the B&B spilling out onto the garden and she began to run towards it. She pushed open the door, and saw one or two people in the communal area, flicking through books, chatting, or cradling cups of tea. Life... lovely, glorious, understandable Island life.

Her mam was in the kitchen and looked up as she came in. 'Had a good night, love?' she asked her.

Christine smiled. There was no getting anything past her mam, really. 'I've had better,' she said, 'but I'm home. So that's the main thing, isn't it?'

'It is, love, it is,' smiled her mam. 'Fancy a cuppa? Kettle's just boiled.'

***

The next morning, half-reluctantly, Christine wandered down to the fields. She discovered that the field was empty and the grass was flattened and muddy where the VW had been. No other trace of the man remained. She breathed out a little sigh of relief. If she was really, totally honest, she was quite pleased that he had disappeared; and she had no desire to ever meet him again.

Present Day

Guy sat in the lounge at the B&B and picked up the newspaper again. He had created a monster over a century ago, and only since the 1960s had he felt some responsibility for Veva's actions. So far, he had never managed to predict where she would attack. Her preferred hunting grounds had always appeared to be England, but once he'd started his research, he had a feeling that she must have lived in Paris at some point. He often wondered if it was her, whenever there had been a spate of unexplained deaths or suicides. Veva had been clever, though; from initially attacking groups of people, she had altered her method and now seemed to pick off men, one by one. That was, he had to admit, more calculating and, it had to be said, less suspicious to the outside world. He had sat down recently and worked out a pattern, spreading a map across the floor and plotting what he thought were her movements.

He blamed the 'sixties' for his guilt. People said if you could remember the sixties, you weren't there. He had been there. He remembered everything. He remembered this island and the girl he had met here. She would never know how lucky she had been. Guy remembered the Priory and the feeling that had swept through his body like a physical pain as he recalled his past life. It was a legend in his society that the Holy Water was there. He already had the dagger, and he had decided, all those years ago, to find the water. It made sense, he told himself, to destroy them both. Then his kind would be safe and he would become the legend. But he had never imagined how this place would make him feel. He had left his estate, and disappeared, buying a VW bus and keeping moving until the likes of Clara stopped looking for him. He had, as they say, re-invented himself.

Guy regretted many things; but he especially regretted Veva. He had never changed anyone since and despite what he was, he couldn't risk a creature like that walking the earth again and much of it was born of a fear that he would be annihilated by something of his own creation. He had watched the statistics crop up in little clusters, moving north from London and heading towards the coast. He had a feeling that she was around here somewhere. These recent drownings off the coast of Lindisfarne were too neat. She had perhaps found a perfect way to cover her tracks – people came here to escape from real life, maybe even just as tourists, like that backpacker who had died recently. So Guy had taken a room on the Island, specifically looking for a Bed and Breakfast that might be owned by the girl who had taken him to the Priory over forty years ago. He wanted to repay her somehow. It had shocked him to see her now – in his mind, she would always be twenty. But she seemed happy and he was glad. He could never quite get used to how people aged. That was something he did not have to concern himself with. And he knew Veva would still be young and beautiful and very, very dangerous.

Almost involuntarily, he clutched the edges of the paper. He had come up here expecting once again to be late, but now he thought about it – he might just be in time. He had seen that group of boys come to the Island and wondered whether it would coax her out. She would relish the challenge. And what could be easier than letting one of them 'drown'? Young men, alcohol and deep water were never a good combination. He remembered the boy in the corridor this morning. I won't be around for one thing. Well, not until later. Maybe.

Guy swore. That was it. She had already started. He scraped the chair back and threw the newspaper on the table. He raced out into the street and looked around him, his keen eyes seeing clearly through the darkness. Eventually, he saw the boy's room-mate meandering through the street, his hands in his pockets. In an instant, Guy was next to him.

The boy jumped. 'Sorry, mate, didn't see you there!' he said, trying to walk past him.

Guy stepped in front of him. 'Where's your friend?' he asked. The boy shrugged his shoulders. 'Your room mate? I need to see him about something.'

'Who? Lucas? Dunno. Around somewhere. In a pub, maybe? With that girl he met?'

'What did she look like?' Guy asked. He could remember Veva's dark hair and even darker eyes as if it was yesterday.

Drew shrugged again. 'Dunno. Ginger, I think. Never gone for Gingers myself.' He pronounced the word *Gin-ga*. Guy stood back. Maybe it wasn't her after all. Then the boy laughed. 'I liked her friend better.'

'What?' Guy interrupted, instantly on his guard again. 'She had a friend with her?'

'Yes. Sorry, no it wasn't a friend.' He thought for a moment, screwing his face up. Guy restrained himself from shaking the boy. He wasn't sure if he was being deliberately obstreperous 'That's it,' the boy said suddenly. 'They were sisters. The dark one was better. I wanted to catch him before he left, ask him to set me up on a date with her. Shame I missed him...'

'Thank you,' Guy cut him short. 'Stay away from those girls. I have to go and find your friend.'

The boy opened his mouth to speak, but Guy was off, running down the street.

'The pubs are that way!' called the boy after him. Guy didn't answer. He was heading to the beach - a storm was blowing up, the causeway would be covered and he had a very good idea where to start looking for Lucas. He felt the weight of the dagger bounce against his hip as he ran. It was secure and he knew what he had to do.

The house looked perfect. The evening sun was bathing the lawn with a golden light and the remnants of the picnic tea lay on the blankets, ready for the maids to remove. Soon, the glasses of champagne would appear and the guests would wander out into the grounds before dinner was served.

'Will they remember us?' the dark-haired girl asked, hanging back as her companion got out of the sleek, green sports car.

'I would imagine so,' replied the other girl. The sun tinted her bobbed curls with copper lights. She stretched like a cat. 'Come along, darling,' she said. 'This is the place.'

'I know it's the place,' said the dark one. 'It looks so familiar.'

'Well, by eight o'clock, they won't even know what they're doing here, never mind us. We just have to wait.' She turned to her friend and her sapphire blue eyes hardened. 'Let me talk.'
The dark girl pouted her perfect, cupid's bow lips. 'Why don't you trust me?' she asked.

'It's too important, sweetheart. It has to be me.'

The dark girl slid gracefully out of the car and padded silently behind the red-head.
'You should have let me cut your hair,' said the red-head. 'It's modern.'

'I don't care.' The dark-haired girl wore her hair in a dishevelled bun and strands were escaping everywhere. She pushed a silver comb in more securely. 'What will you tell them? Oh! Oh look. That's him, isn't it?' She put a hand on the girl's shoulder, stopping her firmly as a young man in tennis whites sauntered around the front of the house whistling. He threw the racquet onto an ornate, white seat and ran up the front staircase. The door was wide open and he disappeared inside. 'He's changed a little,' she said, more to herself than to her companion.

'I believe it is him,' said the red-head. 'That's Leo, darling, try to remember that.' A small, self-satisfied smile played on her lips. 'Good evening, Leo,' she murmured. 'Enjoy it, won't you? We will.'

***

Leo Hartley swaggered through the hallway, peering into the open rooms as he passed them. The drawing room was his least favourite room of the whole place. That was where they reckoned the murder had taken place – still, he thought, had his dear old relation-somewhat-removed not been dallying with the wrong sort of girl, he wouldn't have been killed by her; and he, Leo Hartley, would have remained some obscure cousin and never inherited the place. Leo looked up at the portrait of the young, arrogant-looking William John Hartley as he walked past, and nodded at it. Hartside and all its associated wealth had passed through the mother's side after the murder; there being no male Hartley relatives to bear the name. It had landed in his father's hands eventually; the only proviso being the family changed their name to Hartley to accommodate the inheritance terms. There had been no objection. His father had died during the early part of the Great War and Leo had hardly known him, to be honest. And thus, he had inherited the place. He had also inherited a fair amount of female interest along with it; the genetic mix of the Hartleys was very good. He had the reputation as one of the wealthiest and best-looking young men in London. He had never known that girls could be so forthright. He had spent quite a bit of time in the Capital, and the whole ethos of the Bright Young People was enchanting. Drink, drugs, girls and parties; it was a marvellous lifestyle.

Leo lived and breathed society – and tonight was no exception. The invitation had gone out, Leo thought, somewhere around two a.m. at a costume ball three weeks ago. He had been entranced by a dark-haired girl who had sat on the floor; a vision in a blue, Victorian ball dress. Her eyes were somewhat glassy and unfocussed and she stared at him strangely while he tried to talk to her. It was difficult to articulate the words he wanted after several bottles of champagne, but she didn't seem to mind. She was probably as blotto as he was: inebriated, no less.

'So yes,' he had burbled, 'I own an absolutely enormous property. If I wasn't so spifflicated I could probably drive us there within a couple of hours…but I say, it hasn't stopped me in the past if you're up for it.'

The girl had continued staring at him. 'I think I know you,' she'd said softly. 'Have we met?'

'Possibly. Maybe. Hell, how should I know?' He had laughed and slumped down next to her.

She had never taken her eyes off him, as if she was drilling deep into his mind. 'What year is it?' she had asked. 'What are we doing here?' Then she looked down, as if seeing her dress for the first time. Her fingers twitched and she dug her nails into one of the taffeta frills on the skirt. Carefully, she began to tear it off, concentrating on the material and seeming to forget where she was.

'I say, baby, don't do that!' said Leo, laughing. 'I can wait, you know. Come back to the mews house. There's room there; we don't have to do it here.'

'Mews house?' she said, looking up. 'What's wrong with the summer house?'

'Well, if you come to Hartside, you can see the summer house,' he had wheedled. 'In fact, I'm having a blow there in a couple of weeks. Why don't you come?'

The girl's head snapped up. 'Hartside?' she said, her voice suddenly stronger. She moved quickly and she was on her knees in front of him. 'I do know you. I've been there.' She started to laugh. 'I can remember you very well.'

'Well, that's just swanky!' he said. 'You see, we were meant to be together.'

'Yes we were,' she said and she wrapped her arms around his neck, smiling.

'Jenny, darling, leave him alone,' said a quiet, authoritative voice. 'Not tonight, sweetheart.' This Jenny-girl had looked up and Leo had followed her glance. Another girl stood there, wearing a flowing, ballerina costume exactly like something Isadora Duncan would wear. She even stood like a dancer, her feet poised just so. Her red hair was piled up on her head with a white ribbon wound through it and her eyes were the brightest blue Leo had ever seen.

'Well, hello, doll!' he said smiling at her. 'How well do you girlies know each other? Why is it "not tonight, sweetheart"? Did you have other plans?' He laughed loudly and pulled away from Jenny. 'Can you count me in?'

'I would simply adore that,' said the dancer, 'but I'm afraid I have other plans for you. Another time, maybe?' She smiled at him and blew him a little kiss. 'When is this simply marvellous party you mentioned to my sister?'

'What? Oh – did you hear that?' he said. The girl was moving in and out of focus now, the champagne and the cocaine beginning to take effect.

'I heard everything,' smiled the dancer. 'I'm Cass. And you are...?'

'I am, myself, no less than Leo Hartley,' he said.

115

'*Leo* Hartley?' said Jenny. 'But...'

'Come along, darling,' said Cass and helped Jenny to her feet.

Jenny bent down, apparently to take her shoes off. She tossed them to one side and stood up again, swaying unsteadily. She pulled one hair pin out after another and her hair tumbled down around her shoulders. She swept it angrily to one side and began it claw her fingers through it, brushing it out with her nails. 'Hartley,' she murmured, then reached up to the young man. She wound her arms around his neck again. 'One last time, my love,' she said and kissed him. Leo started to laugh.

'This "do" gets better and better!' he said. 'I shall see you on...yes. On the 26th. Be there.'

'Most definitely,' said Cass. She smiled at him and winked. 'Are you inviting both of us? I hope you won't decide later you've only got time for one of us?'

'Never!' said Leo. It was his turn to sway. 'I've always got time for lookers like you.' The room started to spin and he groped behind him for a chair. Precariously, he sat down on it and watched the girls sashay out of the room. Jenny picked her skirt up and seemed to revel in the swishing material, whereas Cass almost glided. Leo was looking forward to the twenty sixth. At least that seemed to be his thoughts before he passed out.

∗∗∗

The red-head approached the house and shouted through the open door. 'Leo! Leo, darling, are we in the right place for the blow?'

A blonde girl balancing a cigarette in a silver holder popped out of a side-room and looked the pretty red-head up and down. She took in her glitzy, fringed frock and the strings of pearls hanging down to her waist. Surprisingly, she smiled. 'I say, I don't think we've had the pleasure? Dear Leo acquires ladies wherever he goes – I'm sure we will have seen each other in passing, but I can't recall your name?'

'I'm Cass,' said the red-head. She held her hand out to the blonde girl. 'I remember you from the fancy dress ball. Weren't you Marie Antoinette?'

The blonde girl laughed, the tinkling sound bell-like. 'My, how observant you are, Cass. Yes, that's very true. I was indeed Marie Antoinette.' She dropped a theatrical curtsey. 'I'm better known as Jemima.'

'It's a pleasure, Jemima,' smiled Cass.

'I'm Leo's girlfriend,' she said. 'Well, one of his girlfriends. It's the lifestyle you know – one can't be too keen on monogamy. In fact, monogs are so - *blaah*.' She pulled a face.

'You're his girlfriend?' That came from the other girl.

Cass took hold of her hand and pulled her close. 'This is my sister, Jenny,' said Cass.

'Oh. Marvellous to meet you as well, Jenny,' said Jemima. She held her hand out to her. 'We can be Jenny and Jem; what fun!' Jenny stared at her without smiling. The dress she wore was made of black lace and had chiffon drapes attached to the waist. The drapes fell down, skimming her narrow hips and forming a handkerchief-style skirt. She made no move to shake Jemima's hand, and the blonde girl's smile faltered.

She dropped her hand and turned back to Cass. 'Come along in, then. Leo's around here somewhere,' she said. She flicked the cigarette ash into a nearby vase and headed along the corridor, peeping into rooms and calling his name. She turned to see that the newcomers were following her and saw Jenny hanging back, then wander into the drawing room. Jemima tutted under her breath. This one was clearly still recovering from some party or other. 'Jenny!' she shouted. 'This way, please!' She turned to speak to Cass and saw the other girl looking pale and ill. Oh God, not another one that was going to vomit all over the rugs. 'Cass – are you quite well?' she enquired.

'Yes, thank you. It's just – well, it's a little oppressive in here after outside, that's all. Jemima, darling, could you retrieve my sister please? I don't want to go anywhere we shouldn't be.' She smiled again, but Jemima could tell it was forced.

'It's an open house, sweetpea,' said Jemima shrugging. 'She's welcome to go in; just she won't find us later on.'
'She will,' replied Cass. 'We've been here once before – eons ago, it seems.' She narrowed her eyes at Jemima. 'Long before you were on the scene.'

Jemima felt slightly miffed. She decided to ignore that comment. 'Then if that's the case, we should just go on ahead without her,' she said tightly. She flounced away.

Just as Jemima approached the bottom of the grand staircase, a man came down the stairs limping and leaning on a polished wooden cane. He seemed to be in his late twenties and had a thin, haunted face. He was a good-looking young man despite that, and his brown hair flopped engagingly down over one eye.

His face lit up as he saw Jemima coming towards them. 'Jemima!' he said. 'That's where you are. I've been searching for you.'

'Stephen!' replied Jemima, blushing beneath her face powder. 'I'm just welcoming some new friends to Hartside. Leo knows them. I seem to have lost one of them on my way though.'

'I'm here,' said Jenny. Jemima jumped. Jenny was standing behind her, looking at her oddly. 'Some things never change,' Jenny said. She looked past Jemima towards the portrait of Leo's long-lost relative. She made a small *aaah* sound under her breath and walked past Jemima towards it.

'Jenny,' said Cass. There was a warning in her voice. 'Come along, darling. We've so much to do before the fun starts.'

'Now isn't that a wonderful portrait,' said Jenny. 'Why, I think I've seen some pictures like that before.' She reached her hand out and tenderly traced it down the side of the man's face. 'Will Hartley.' She smiled and tilted her head to one side. 'Hello, darling.' Then she laughed. She turned to Cass, her eyes dancing with excitement. 'I'm so looking forward to the party!' she said. 'Are you going to introduce us to your friend?' She held her hand out to Stephen.

Stephen smiled and took it. 'Stephen Masters' he said. 'Late of the Royal Sussex Regiment.'

'Stephen was in the R.A.F. during the War,' said Jemima. She linked his free arm, proprietarily; the one he leaned on his stick.

'Afraid I left a chunk of my leg behind,' he said. He loosened his grip on Jenny's hand. 'At least it got me out of the War.'

'Stephen writes poetry, don't you sweetie?' said Jemima. Casually, she manoeuvred herself in between him and Jenny. 'We're great friends. Very lucky he came back to us.' She looked up at him adoringly. 'Very lucky indeed.'

Stephen met her gaze and his eyes softened. 'Indeed,' he said. 'Jem and I go back years. Always thought we'd be together at some point in the future. Hey ho, that's how it goes.' He smiled ruefully.

'Now darling, don't be like that,' scolded Jemima. 'You left me.' She pouted. 'Can I help it if Leo came along in those awful years?'

'I couldn't hope to compete with him,' said Stephen.

118

Jemima tinkled out a laugh. 'Naughty boy,' she said, tapping him on the nose. 'It's not the money...' She bit her tongue. The two girls stared at her in silence and she tucked a strand of hair behind her ear and cleared her throat. 'Anyway. Leo should be here. Probably lounging around before dinner.' She let go of Stephen's arm and pushed open a door. The man in the tennis whites lay sprawled across a chaise longue, an empty bottle lying on the table next to him. Jemima shook him roughly and he opened one eye.

'Jemmy-emmy-ima!' he slurred. 'Marvellous girl. Come here.' He reached up and tried to hook his arms around her waist.

'Visitors, darling,' she said. 'Two girlies you might know.'

He sat up and stared at them, a light dawning in his eyes. 'I say!' he cried. 'I've one of each tonight: a blonde, a red-head and a brunette.' He laughed and squeezed Jemima. 'Is Stephen here? We did invite him, didn't we?'

'We did,' she confirmed. 'He's here.' She looked around but Stephen had disappeared, the faint tap-tap of his cane moving through the corridors of Hartside. 'Well, he was here. Anyway, we'll leave you to it. Don't forget to change, you naughty man,' she said. She pulled another cigarette out of a stand on the table and inserted it in her holder. She leaned over and lit it from a smouldering stub in the ashtray on the table beside the empty bottle.

'Excellent,' said Leo. He lay back down and pulled a cushion over his head. 'Ten minutes. That's all I ask. Ten minutes...' He apparently dozed off and Jenny looked down at him in some distaste.

'He seemed rather lively outside,' she commented.

Jemima tapped her forefinger to her temple. 'It's the stuff he takes,' she replied. 'Uppers, downers, you name it.' Then she smiled. 'I'll get you some. They're fabulous.'

***

Jenny drifted into Cass's room just before dinner time.

'It's just as I remember,' she said in wonder. She sat down carefully on the bed and smoothed the covers out next to her. Cass was standing by the window.

She glared at Jenny. 'At least this isn't the room,' she said. 'That would have been too much to bear.' Jenny shrugged her shoulders and stood up. She wandered over to the window and twitched the curtains. A few people were milling about the garden and brays of laughter drifted up through the evening air.

119

'They disgust me,' said Jenny. 'I hate them all.' She turned to Cass. 'It has to be tonight.' Then her demeanour changed and she smiled. 'Did you see his portrait?' she said softly. 'When do you think it was painted?'

'Why do you care?' snapped Cass. 'It's something I never want to see again. I've tried for years to forget his face.'

'He was handsome, you must agree,' said Jenny. She reached over and hugged Cass. 'But it's in the past. We have each other.' It was the most animated Cass had seen Jenny for a while.

There was a knock at the door, and Jenny darted over to open it. Jemima stood there, draped in a scarlet sheath dress, the obligatory cigarette had been replaced by a half-empty champagne bottle. She had painted a perfect cupid's bow to match Jenny's on her own, rather narrow, lips and smiled at her guests. 'Are you coming down?' she slurred. 'Leo is wondering where you are.'

'Hasn't he got enough to keep him occupied?' asked Jenny.

'I'm sure he has,' replied Jemima, 'but he has specifically asked me to come and find you. There's a group of us at the pool, if you want to join us. Or you could grab a drink and join in the conversation. The dancing will start soon. Someone's just gone to find a gramophone. It's all very *blaah* at the minute.' She rolled her eyes and took a swig from the bottle. 'Hopefully it will pick up soon.' Jenny looked at Cass.

Cass shook her head imperceptibly. She moved towards the open door and covered Jenny's hand. 'We'll start at the pool,' she said. 'Where's your boyfriend?'

'Leo?' asked Jemima. She shook her head, the blonde waves never moving, so lacquered in place were they. 'God knows where he is by now.' She leaned into the girls. 'I bet you two will flush him out. He did ask for you.'

Cass laughed. 'No darling, your other boyfriend,' she said.

Jemima paused for a minute, a strange little look fleeting across her face. 'Oh. You mean Stephen. Is it that obvious?' She smirked. 'He's along the corridor. Just a few rooms along.' She gestured with the bottle. 'I'm flushing him out next. You can amuse Leo while I'm occupied. Darling Leo is my umbrella, all the girls know that.'

'Excuse me?' asked Cass. 'What on earth does that mean?'

'Oh sweetie, if you're going to be regulars at our parties, you need to learn the lingo,' said Jemima. 'An umbrella, darling, is a young man that you can borrow for the evening.' She winked. 'He's not spanking new, though. He's been through quite a few showers.' She laughed and blew them a kiss. 'Oh – those pills I promised you. There should be some in the drawers. If not, there's plenty outside. Just ask anyone.' She swanned off along the corridor, bumping into an elegant table on her way.

'I hate her,' muttered Jenny. 'I think I hate her the most. She has the morals of an alley cat. They all do. I don't know about the flying one?'

'He has to go too. He's part of it. But it's Leo for me,' said Cass. 'He's the one I want.'

'Darling, he looks just like Will,' said Jenny, opening her eyes wide.

'All the more reason,' replied Cass bitterly. Suddenly, the shutters went down in Jenny's eyes and she began to hum a little tune; slightly off-key and very quietly. Cass knew she'd lost her again. This was the best time, though, when she was like this. She became a killing machine.

Psychopaths were like that.

***

The newspapers had a field day when they discovered the carnage. Nobody could agree how many people had been involved – it was clearly a gang, they said. No one person could do that. And surely, if it was one person, then they would easily have been overpowered by the partygoers? There were so many drugs and so much booze in the house and the gardens, that one theory was that they had all been served a lethal cocktail: the cocktail had sedated them enough to make them unresisting. Every one of them had chunks of flesh ripped from their bodies – all at main arterial points. The majority of the injuries were to the throats. One of the more outrageous ideas suggested was that a team of vampires had gatecrashed the party: which was, of course, ridiculous. One of the victims was a War veteran. He was found cradling the naked body of Miss Jemima Saunders-Townsend, the fiancée of the householder, Leo Hartley. Once the shock waves of the murders had faded from society, gossips began speculating. The veteran had allegedly had such a look of horror on his face that people wondered whether Leo had found them. But of course, that was ridiculous as well, because, like most of that set, Leo knew all about it.

121

Present Day

Guy had underestimated Veva; he would even admit that he had been stupid. He pounded across the scrubby grass towards the lime kilns, his sharp eyes scanning the horizon for her.

He spotted the dark figure diving into the sea. He saw the wind lift her dark hair and her slim figure disappear beneath the waves. In an instant, he was in the water, striking out effortlessly against the current to reach her. He was a strong swimmer – stronger than she was. So focussed was she on her quarry, that she didn't hear him above the storm until he was close behind her. She whipped her head around, her hair slapping through the water, and saw him just as he reached out and closed his fingers around the top of her arm. She pulled against him, but he held her fast. He dragged her towards the shore and across the sharp shale, up onto a slope of the beach. She writhed, trying to escape, but he held her down.

'Don't even try to get away!' he hissed. 'I know who you are and what you do.'

'Let me go!' she shouted. 'I don't know you! Get off me!' She thrashed her head from side to side, squeezing her eyes shut. 'Get off! Leave me alone! I have to go!'

'Where are you going, Veva?' he asked.

She shrieked and tried to wriggle free from his grasp. 'I don't know you, I don't know you...' she kept repeating. 'I'm not Veva. I'm not her.'

'You do know me, Genevieve.'

'I don't, I don't know you. I don't know any Genevieves. I'm not Veva. She's dead. She died when Will died...' The girl opened her eyes and glared at Guy. 'He's dead. He was killed.' Then she started laughing. 'I think I killed him, you know. It might have been me. She said it was...'

'Who was it?' he repeated. 'Who said that?'

'Nobody. Nobody at all.' She struggled to throw him off, but his hands tightened. 'No. It wasn't her. She didn't tell me.' She suddenly growled at him, a low, guttural noise that startled even Guy. 'I saw him. She showed me.' She bared her teeth and tried to bite him, defending herself. Guy held her tighter; she was completely insane and even more dangerous than he had anticipated. 'Get off me, Joseph!' she cried. 'Get off me...' Her body suddenly went limp.

'Joseph?' She stared at Guy, as if seeing him clearly for the first time. 'You're not Joseph,' she murmured. 'I do know you though.' She struggled to focus and Guy saw a different kind of madness in her eyes. Suddenly, they hardened and she opened them wide. 'Montgomery!' A giggle started somewhere deep inside of her and then she burst out laughing. 'Damn you, Guy Montgomery. I can remember you. Tell me,' she said, 'did I ever thank you properly, Sir Guy? Aren't you proud of me? Look at what you created! I have you to thank for this. You saved my life; no, you gave me life. I am forever in your debt. Eternally.' She laughed again. 'I'm so proud of *me!*'

'There's nothing to be proud of!' Guy fired back.

She wriggled and he held her down. 'Let me go!' she shouted again. 'I'm not telling you anything else. I *am* proud of myself. I've done all this *myself.*'

Guy bared his fangs. 'I know there is someone else. Who is it? Who's the red-head?' He saw her fight within herself, torn between admitting he was right or claiming all the mis-placed glory for herself.

Then suddenly her attitude shifted again and she glared at him, full of hatred. 'You don't know me; you know nothing about me. But I am not a liar. That's one of the things Joseph called me and I never lied!'

'I didn't say you were lying.' Guy forced himself to soften his voice, to cajole her into confessing. 'I want to know how clever you are.' The words choked him. 'How clever you both are. Who is your friend?'

'All right,' she sighed theatrically, 'I'll confess. It's nice to be told I'm clever. I have a friend, but you'll never work out who it is. I bet you don't. We go a long way back. We've got so much in common.' She giggled.

'But who is it?' yelled Guy.

'You already know!' she screamed back. 'I told you! Why can't you remember?' Her voice changed into a whine, making her sound like a spoiled child. 'Who else had Will hurt? Who else had he deceived?'

'I'm not here to play games with you!' Guy snapped, losing patience. 'Tell me who it is. No-one else need die.'

'Oh, so now you're all penitent and good, are you?' she sneered. 'That's not what we are, you taught me that. Why, you encouraged me to kill my brother. Can you remember that?'

'I tried to save you,' said Guy. 'You told me yourself it would have been suicide to return home. I tried to give you an escape route but it doesn't mean I don't regret doing it. I've changed since then. But you - you'd murdered two people, Veva!' You...' Suddenly, he realised.

Veva started to laugh, a low, mocking laugh. 'Oh, very *good*, Sir Guy,' she said. 'You've worked it out. I say, well done that man. Only I'm not Veva anymore. I told you. She's gone. I'm Jenny now. Genevieve or Veva or whoever she was died when Will did. He deserved it though, for what he did... '

'So it was the girl,' interrupted Guy. 'His fiancée...'

'Don't *say* that word!' screeched Veva. 'You've made me very sad, Sir Guy. Why are you here? Why can't you just leave me alone? Go on – go off to Hartside and see what you can find. He might still be there. Tell him I said hello. In fact, give him my love...'

Guy could tell her was losing her again. He had to speak quickly. 'Will's fiancée,' he repeated. 'What did you do to her? Why?'

Veva wriggled again, trying to release her shoulders from his grasp. The shutters lifted for a moment. 'That girl was alive when I went back, I didn't kill her properly when I killed Will,' she muttered. 'I tried to do it again. But I didn't do it properly - again.' She glared up at Guy. 'I knew then that she wasn't meant to die. She was meant to help me. But it didn't *work*!' cried Veva as Guy held her firmly. 'She just wouldn't *die*. So she had to come with me.' She laughed. 'She feels the same way I do. Will made fools out of us both. Men can't be trusted, can they? Just look at my brother.'

'There was no need to do all of this,' said Guy. 'I can't believe I didn't anticipate it.'

'You just didn't know me very well, did you?' laughed Veva. 'My brother always told me I was evil. My mother hated me for the way I looked, but Joseph knew my soul was as dark as his. It's such a shame you didn't know sooner, Guy. Cass was with me when I met Joseph at the chapel. It was fun.'

'Nobody drowned here, did they?' asked Guy.

'Clever boy,' hissed Veva, 'They did not. We have been tidying up a little. Cass plans it out. She researches it. She identifies who deserves it. Every one of those men – they've all used women and tossed them aside like they were worthless. And me? I just enjoy myself. She won't let me do anything, she won't let me, Guy…tell her. Tell her when you see her. But I think she likes this one. I think she does. But I like him too, it's just not fair…'

'Where is he?' said Guy, cutting her off.

'Oh, he's safe. Cass is looking after him.' Veva began to laugh. 'In fact, you've delayed me, Sir Guy. Maybe he's not so safe anymore. Who knows? Cass isn't my responsibility. I can't tell her what to do. It depends if he upsets her. She'll wait a while then she might just go for it herself. Now wouldn't that be tragic? Well, it would be for me.' She pouted. 'I quite enjoy it. I'm rather good at it now. I've had lots of practice since we last met.' She bared her fangs at Guy. 'I have you to thank for giving me the gift.'

'Cass is your responsibility!' cried Guy. 'She didn't have a choice in what she became. Where is she?'

'Not telling,' sniffed Veva. Guy shook her in frustration. He threw her aside, and she tumbled into a heap, laughing. Her long, dark hair was matted with sand and she rolled over on the beach to sit up.

'I will find them,' swore Guy, 'and I'll stop them. But first…' Guy moved so quickly, that by the time the blade of the silver dagger plunged into her body, Veva had no time to react. She opened her eyes in shock and collapsed back onto the sand, staring sightlessly at the sky. Guy dived back into the ocean, not waiting to watch the body quietly disintegrate and merge with the shale on the beach.

***

Guy could see the refuge looming out of the waves, dirty white against the dark sky. The door was banging open and Guy fixed his gaze on it. His keen senses picked up two people inside the building. He saw two shapes, one tall with slightly rounded shoulders – a young man in an attitude of dejection, and a young woman - small and slim - carefully blocking the entrance. He saw her arm reach out and carefully pull the door shut. A rowing boat bobbed around the base of the refuge, moored inexpertly to one of the legs.

Guy reached the bottom of the refuge and pulled himself up onto the few stairs that remained out of the water. He listened carefully; he could still hear them moving around inside.

'Oh, I'm really sorry you had to come all the way out here to get me. Take your jacket off, it must be damp.' That was the girl speaking. 'At least we're quite safe in here for the time being. It's not too bad, anyway, is it?' A pause – he could imagine her looking around the interior of the building. 'At least Jenny didn't try to come. I would have worried about her rowing out here.' A sigh. 'I hope she's all right. Anyway,' the girl laughed, 'it gives us some time together, doesn't it?'

'I suppose so.' That was the boy.

'What? You don't sound that sure. What's up?' That was the girl again. 'Oh. Oh no. She didn't, did she? Did she kiss you? She's always doing that. She's always trying to take men off me. Tell me you didn't fall for it...' Silence. 'You did. Oh Lucas.' She sounded sad. 'You fell for it. You've messed up again haven't you? Just like how you messed up with Laura. That's really upset me...'

Guy had, by now, reached the top step and the doorway. He pulled hard on the handle and the door swung open. He was greeted by the sight of two people, the girl with her back to him, and the boy facing him. The boy looked up as Guy entered, his face registering shock. The girl spun around, and then she too looked astonished. Her mood suddenly altered.

'Who are you?' she snapped.

'Well clearly I'm not Jenny,' growled Guy. 'Sorry to disappoint you.'

***

Lucas stared at the man who had just burst into the refuge. He was dripping wet and appeared outraged. He glared at Cass with such accusation in his eyes that even Lucas felt uncomfortable.

'Woah!' Lucas said. He put a protective hand out. 'Leave her alone, whoever you are.'

The man ignored him and continued staring at Cass. 'She told me everything,' he said. 'I know what you're planning.'

To Lucas' surprise, Cass started to laugh. 'Oh, you're funny,' she said, 'but I don't think I've had the pleasure?' She moved towards him. 'I'm sure if you were to introduce yourself, I might remember if I had ever heard of you?'

'Guy Montgomery,' said the man. 'I knew Genevieve a very long time ago. Has that jogged your memory?'

'Guy Montgomery? *You!* said Cass. 'You're the one? Well, in that case, I have much to thank you for, Sir Guy.' She curtsied prettily. 'If Jenny had never met you, we'd all have gone to our graves happy by now.' Her face suddenly changed. She glared at him and narrowed her eyes. 'But I digress. Where is she?'

126

'In Hell, I hope,' said the man. Suddenly, he lunged at Cass and she darted out of his way. Lucas saw a faint gleam of silver in the man's waistband as he moved, and so, it seemed, did Cass.

'You used that?' she cried. It was the first time Lucas had seen fear in her face. 'How did you get that? It's a myth!'

'It's not a myth,' said Guy. Lucas recognised him now as the man from his B&B – the one who had spoken to him that morning. 'I have proved that with Veva tonight, and I shall prove it to you as well. Lucas - get out of here now!'

Lucas started – how the hell did he know his name? 'What's going on?' he cried. He ran at the man, intending to push him out of the way, but this Guy or whatever his name was, stretched out a hand and literally stopped Lucas in his tracks. Lucas caught his breath as the man held him at arm's length, his fingers splayed across his chest.

'Go!' the man shouted. It was clear, now the man's waist was exposed, that the silver object was a dagger of some sort. 'This isn't a woman, it's a vampire,' he said. 'Get away, let me deal with her...'

Cass howled and she threw herself at Guy. Guy grappled with her, and they both fell to the floor. A small bottle rolled out of Guy's pocket and bounced towards Lucas.

'Lucas! For God's sake, get out of here,' yelled the man again. He rolled over and tried to grab the bottle, but as he did so, the girl flung herself on top of him, pinning him down.

She laughed, a vile, evil laugh that went on and on. 'At the end, she did what I told her. She created me, but she couldn't tame me. It was me who decided what we did. Me. She made me hate her, you know; all the men loved her more. All of them, except you. Thank you, Sir Guy. That was the only good thing about you.' Then, to Lucas' horror, he saw a flash of silver as Cass ripped the dagger from Guy's belt and plunged it into his body. There was a whooshing noise and the girl rolled onto her back, still laughing as the man crumbled into dust.

Lucas felt sick. He turned and seized the door handle, his heart banging in his chest. He tried to pull the door open – he would jump into the sea rather than stay here another minute. The girl laughed and sprang to her feet. She grabbed Lucas by the arm and pulled him away from the door as if he were thistledown. He landed with a crash at the other side of the room.

Cass threw the dagger into the opposite corner where it landed with a clatter. 'You won't be needing that!' she hissed. She crouched down, ready to attack him.

Lucas gasped as Cass leapt forward. The dagger lay in the corner taunting him. He knew that however fast he moved, she would move faster. She seized him by the shoulder as he lay there and pulled him close to her. Her grip was like a vice. He struggled and writhed as she held him effortlessly, digging her fingers into his shoulder blade.

She brought her other arm around as if she was going to embrace him and suddenly she was in front of him, laughing at the fear in his face. 'I'd make it quick,' she hissed, 'but really, it's more fun to do it slowly. You should have thought about Laura, shouldn't you? Before you did *that*. And thought about *me* before you kissed *her*.' She brought her face close to his shoulder and punctured his skin with her fangs.

***

Lucas screamed out in pain. He had never been so terrified in his entire life. He felt venom pumping into his bloodstream, enough to make his veins burn, but then, like a gunshot, a voice shouted in his ear.

'*The Holy Water! Use the Holy Water!*' Lucas opened his eyes wide, catching his breath as the burning subsided. A white mist was forming behind Cass – the shape grew until it filled the corner of the room and Lucas could identify the outline of a man. Cass appeared to be oblivious to the voice and the figure behind her. Instead, she took pleasure in ripping open Lucas's shirt and came down to sink her teeth into the top of his chest.

Lucas screamed again as more venom pumped into his system. She was moving closer to his heart, he realised. He wasn't going to survive many more of these. His legs were going weak and his vision was blacking out. Cass appeared to be delighted. She let go of him and he collapsed onto the floor. He rolled into a ball, his breath coming in jagged gasps. He forced open his eyes and his gaze settled on the small bottle which had fallen out of the man's pocket.

'*Use it!*' said the voice again, more urgently. '*Quickly. You don't have much time. It's Holy Water. I blessed it. Use it, for God's sake!*' The curl of Lucas' body hid the bottle from the vampire's line of vision and he continued to stare at it.

'How?' croaked Lucas. The bottle was just within his grasp, if he could only stretch his arm out...

'*Break it, throw it at her, anything!*' came the voice. '*For the love of God, just do it.*' Lucas painfully moved his arm and reached out, groping for the bottle. Anything was worth a try. He was dying, he was going mad, or something. But he had to try. Please God this was just a bad dream and he'd wake up at any moment. Lucas edged his fingers out. Just a little more, he thought, just a little more. She was coming back for him one last time; he could hear the boards creaking as she moved towards him. She was in no hurry, it seemed. Lucas assumed she was enjoying herself, spinning it out a little longer, the way a cat toys with a mouse before moving in for the kill.

The shadow moved swiftly to the entrance, and the door of the hut swung open, clashing against the door frame; it was enough to distract Cass. She spun around and Lucas managed to grab the bottle. He raised himself up on one elbow and tried to uncork it. The stopper was stuck fast. He fell back with a groan. It was impossible – he would have to resign himself to dying. Cass turned back to him and moved towards him. She bent down and dragged him to his feet. He swayed, and she smiled at him, affectionately, almost.

'One more kiss, Lucas?' she purred. 'You've been fun. I'll miss you. And, truthfully, I *did* like you.' She leaned in towards him, grabbing him. Lucas had one chance – he took it. He raised his hand in front of his chest as she pulled him sharply towards her, the glass bottle between them.

There was an almighty crack as the old bottle shattered against the inflexibility of Cass's chest, splashing up into her face and soaking her front.

Her eyes widened and she stared at Lucas. 'You bastard!' she hissed. Lucas managed to jump back and crouch down, taking cover as a white flame engulfed Cass's body: then the flame evaporated, taking the vampire with it.

***

Lucas stood breathing heavily, oblivious to the fact that the Holy Water was, similarly, soaking down his bare torso. He looked down and saw the water run over the half-moon bite mark on his chest. Shards of glass were now embedded in his palm, but he cared nothing for the pain; he rubbed at the water with his injured hand, smearing the blood and water together. He became aware of a warmth beginning at the centre of his chest and pumping into the cuts on his hand as the water seeped into the wounds and ran over his skin. Gradually, he felt the strength returning to him and the burning sensation of the venom calm. He saw the dagger lying in the corner of the room, and stumbled over to it. Bending down, he picked it up and weighed it in his hands.

'You will never have cause to use that,' came the voice again. 'Have faith. The Holy Water will protect you now.' Lucas jumped and turned. The white mist was back, but this time a young man seemed to step out of it and fill the refuge with a sense of peace and spirituality.

He smiled at Lucas. 'Well done,' he said. 'I am proud of you.'

'I don't understand...' began Lucas. 'Who are you?'

'That dagger was mine,' said the man. 'My name is Kester Lawson. I had the dagger made to prevent creatures like that from walking the earth. It worked for a time, but I realise now that I still had much to learn. You, my friend, have divine protection. You will not need my dagger to save you.' Lucas stared at the man dumbstruck. The man smiled. 'Do not worry, they won't harm you again.'

'I...I...' stammered Lucas.

The man raised a hand. 'Please. You are safe. But, just for your own peace of mind, you must do two things. You need to go to the Priory with two containers of Holy Water and bury them by the *piscina*.'

'But I don't know what a *piscina* is...' began Lucas. 'And I don't know where to get Holy Water.' It felt surreal answering him – it was like he was talking to someone who wasn't really there. Was he a ghost or something? Lucas shivered. He'd always imagined he'd be scared rigid if he saw a ghost. Christ, this fellow was nothing compared to Cass.

'No "buts",' said Kester Lawson. 'You will find it. We need to replace what the Lord provided for us. And you also need to discard the dagger. Throw it into the sea. It will find its place, I have trust. The Lord will send it on a journey with the tides, and the ocean will take it where it needs to be. I can wait – He has taught me patience. And then I will be able to help the next owner.'

Lucas stared at the hazy figure in front of him. 'What – just throw it away now? Down the steps into the sea?' he asked.

Kester nodded. 'You do not need it,' he said. 'You are not a slayer. That is not your future.'

'A slayer?' cried Lucas. 'Like a vampire slayer? I don't want to be one of those! I don't want anything to do with those things... I didn't even think they existed!'

'You see, that is where we are different,' said Kester. 'I wanted to hunt them down. I wanted to kill every last one of them. You have to be born that way – destined to it. There is no room for anything else in your life when you are a slayer. It would not, I believe, suit you.'

'Damn right!' said Lucas. He stared at the dagger. 'Can I do it now? Can I just get rid of it?'

'You can indeed,' said Kester. 'Then I suggest you take a little time to yourself in here. Gather your thoughts and rest while the tide is high. I will stay with you for a little while if you wish.' He moved over to the corner of the hut and seemed to sit down on the bench. Another wave of peace washed over Lucas, as Kester settled down.

'You don't scare me,' stated Lucas. 'I always thought I'd be scared. But I'm not.'

'There's no reason to fear me,' said Kester. 'Now please, discard the dagger and rest. We have a while, I believe, before the tide goes down.'

'I could get the boat – I could go. What if another one comes here?' said Lucas. He began to panic; a memory washed over him of Cass's face as she bore down on him. 'The other one – Jenny.' He swore. 'Was she one as well...?'

'There are no more vampires here,' replied Kester. 'I swear to you. Now, open the door and throw the dagger away. You are protected.'

'But how do I know I can I trust you?' said Lucas.

Kester looked at him calmly. 'Only you can make that decision,' he said. 'Sometimes, we just have to work on instinct.'

Lucas stared back at Kester. It was the oddest feeling. As he concentrated on the young man's clear, open face, he felt the fear begin to fade. He became aware of the weight of the dagger again and knew without a doubt that what Kester told him was the truth. He moved over to the door and opened it. A gust of sea air rushed in and made him gasp. He took one last look at the dagger and cast it out, away into the sea. It tumbled into the water and was swallowed

131

up in a great wave which rose up to meet it. Lucas saw a flash of silver as it sank into the waves and realised he had been holding his breath. He exhaled and turned to Kester.

The young man nodded. 'Well done,' he said. 'Now rest.' Lucas closed the door behind him and stumbled over to the wooden bench by the wall. He sat down at the opposite end to Kester and exhaustion overcame him. He closed his eyes and rested his head against the wall. 'Why don't you sleep?' asked Kester.

Lucas nodded, still with his eyes closed. 'Good idea,' he mumbled. He lay down and curled up on the bench. He pulled his coat over his shoulders and barely felt the hard, slatted seat beneath him. He was aware instead of the calming, tranquil sensation that emanated from the figure in the corner. 'Will you stay with me?' he asked. His brain was churning with the events of the evening. 'And will you be here when I wake up?' He heard a soft laugh.

'I will stay as long as need be,' said Kester.

'Thanks,' murmured Lucas and gave himself up to sleep.

***

Lucas didn't know how long he had been asleep, but grey, early morning light was leaking through the windows of the refuge when he opened his eyes. He had woken up with a start, not realising at first where he was. As his eyes became accustomed to the milky dawn, the events of the previous evening started to crowd into his conscious mind: the man from the B&B, Cass, a dagger... and Kester. Lucas sat up quickly and looked around the room. The spirit, if that's what it was, had gone. The room felt quiet, though, sort of like how a church felt.

'Hello?' he tried. He listened for an answer – nothing. 'Umm, is anyone there?' Still nothing. He stood up and shrugged his jacket on. He moved towards the door. He pulled it open and stared out. The tide had subsided, and the causeway was just clearing. Three inches of water, maybe four covered the grey ribbon of road which led onto the island. He smelled the salt and the morning air and suddenly felt at peace. His boat was still tied up, half sunk into the sand and he could see a battered old land rover bumping through the water towards the refuge.

'Lucas!' he heard. 'Lucas, mate! Is that you?' Drew was hanging out of the back window, but he couldn't tell who was driving the vehicle. Lucas raised his arm in acknowledgement and waved at his friend. He felt weird – displaced, sort of. Had last night really happened? It didn't seem feasible in the daylight. He turned and looked back at the room. He shivered. The memory of those...things...evaporating and crumbling, pushed back into his mind. The man from the B&B. Had he been one then? A good one? Were there such things? Or had he dreamed it all? He rubbed his chest and felt a slight, half-moon shaped bump. A tiny scar showed up faintly against his skin and he stared at it. It had been real. All of it. He ran his fingers over his shoulder and felt the same little raised mark. His heart began to beat faster and he recalled the terror when Cass had come towards him for the third time. Then, just as quickly, he felt the fear subside and remembered Kester's words - '*You have divine protection now. Have faith.*' He stood up a little straighter and pulled the tattered edges of his shirt together, zipping his jacket up. Thank God he had brought a jacket - he couldn't explain the bloodstains away any time soon. The land rover chugged through the final few metres and Drew jumped out, splashing his way to the refuge steps. Lucas had never seen him look quite so scared and as young as he did at that moment.

'Jesus, Lucas. You been here all night?' Drew asked. 'When you didn't come back, we were all worried. Christ, I haven't slept all night. That bloke's gone as well from the B&B. He didn't come down to breakfast. Hasn't been seen since last night. There were only a couple of things in his room when they checked it as well. No-one travels that light do they? He's vanished. And we all thought you had, well, you know. Thought you'd...' Drew shrugged his shoulders. 'You know, like the paper said.' His voice cracked a little. Lucas tactfully ignored it.

'I'm fine,' said Lucas, stepping back to let Drew into the hut. 'I was supposed to meet someone here last night and she didn't turn up...I got stuck.' He thought quickly. 'Maybe she went off with the bloke from the B&B instead?' He felt sick to the stomach lying to Drew; but what else could he do? He knew for a fact he could never tell anyone what had happened here. Best to let them think they'd both buggered off. Drew's face brightened. Obviously, this seemed to be a simple, non-offensive solution - the sort he liked.

'Yes. That's it. Nice one. Wahey!' The old Drew was back. 'God, wish I could pull one like that. Not a Ginger though. Nah – quite liked the other one. Dunno where she's gone. Maybe with them? The three of them?' In Drew's mind, the question seemed to be happily resolved.

133

'Yeah. Maybe,' said Lucas. 'Can we go now? Can we get a lift back? I need to take the boat back too...' Although he didn't have a clue what to do with the boat – it had been Jenny's, hadn't it? He shivered again.

'Sure, come on,' said Drew. 'Nice place you've got here,' he said and laughed. 'Not quite the warm comfy bed I had last night though.'

'And I want to go to the Priory later,' added Lucas. Drew opened his mouth. 'Alone,' stated Lucas. Drew closed his mouth again and looked insulted. 'Stuff I need to study,' said Lucas. 'Sorry mate.' Drew shrugged.

'Ok, whatever.' The word "study" had clearly put him off. 'You got everything, then we can go? Got your mobile?'

'No mobile,' said Lucas. 'No signal. She said...' He realised it had just been a ploy. To make sure he couldn't call for help - or to make it look like suicide. A chill ran down his back. 'Come on. Let's go.'

'They yours?' asked Drew, nodding towards two small objects on the bench. Lucas moved closer to them - two small, old-fashioned, glass flagons, full of liquid. They looked like they had some sort of white fabric, a ribbon, or a handkerchief or something, stuffed inside them as well.

He paused, staring at them. 'Yes,' he said finally. 'Yes. I'll take them.'

'Good. I'm missing breakfast to come out here,' moaned Drew. He went out of the hut and Lucas followed him down the stairs. They splashed over to the land rover, the wet sand sucking at their feet. The boat was already loaded onto the roof rack and Lucas clambered inside. The landlord from the B&B was driving and his wife was in the passenger seat.

'Thank goodness!' said the landlady. She smiled at him. 'We were worried about you.'

'Thanks for coming for me,' said Lucas.

'We couldn't wait any longer,' she said. 'We don't know where Mr Montgomery has gone...' her voice trailed off. She seemed to be remembering something, then shook her head a little and began to speak again. 'He seems to have disappeared off the face of the earth. He wasn't with you in there was he? No – that's daft. He'd have come out with you, wouldn't he?' Lucas didn't answer.

'The girl Lucas was meant to meet didn't turn up either,' said Drew, nudging his friend and laughing. 'Bet they're together.'

The landlady laughed. 'Yes, that's it. I suppose they left last night. He'll be married or something,' she said, 'The quiet ones are always the worst.' She looked at her silent husband and laughed again. 'Definitely.'

'Thanks, Chris,' muttered her husband, but there was no malice in it.

The vehicle bumped onto dry land and Lucas finally felt able to relax. He saw the Priory a short distance away and leaned forward.

'Do you mind just dropping me here?' he asked the landlord. Brian, he thought he was called. 'I just need to nip over the road for something.'

'Yeah, no problem,' said Brian, and stopped the car.

'Thanks. I'll be back shortly,' he said. He smiled at the landlady. 'I'll be back for breakfast, I won't be long,'

'OK,' she said and Lucas climbed out.

'I'll get on with your bacon while you're gone!' called Drew, as the car pulled away. 'Don't hurry back!' Lucas lifted his hand and watched them drive away. He took the shortcut through the houses he had spotted and hurried over to the early morning Priory. The Island was just beginning to wake up, but he doubted anybody would be at the Priory just yet. Good. There was just that one final thing he had to do, then he wanted to forget this whole business.

***

Lucas climbed over the fence into the Priory grounds. He stood, staring about him, wondering which way he should go. What had Kester told him? The *piscina*? He looked around and his eyes settled on a pale, golden haze somewhere over in the direction where the sun was rising. He wrinkled his nose – was that just the rays of the early morning sun or something else? The ancient stone walls seemed to be bathed in the light and he turned to face the east properly. Well, he had to start somewhere. Maybe there would be an interpretation board up somewhere that would help him if he needed it. He wandered down the length of the silent Priory and, bizarrely, the golden light seemed to draw him closer. Finally, he reached the wall and found himself staring at a small niche, with what looked like a drain in the middle of it. He stepped towards it to inspect it and the soft ground beneath it gave way slightly under his toe. He looked down and saw a small sign fixed onto the bottom of the wall – *Piscina* and *Aumbry*.

Lucas' heart began to beat faster. This was it. Whether it was the sunrise, or Kester, or something else entirely, he knew that he had to bury the phials right here. He crouched down and began scooping the earth away with his fingertips. Soon, there was a hole wide enough to lay the two bottles in, side by side. Lucas placed them carefully together and covered them with the soil.

He patted it down and sat back on his heels. 'I've done it,' he said. 'That's it, isn't it? That was what I was supposed to do?' He looked around him, half-expecting a voice to answer him. Nothing. 'OK. I'll take that as a "yes",' he said. He was beginning to feel a little bit silly, hunched over a pile of earth in a ruined Priory. Then the hairs on the back of his neck began to prickle. He had the feeling that somebody – or something – was creeping up on him, watching him and waiting for his next move. He tensed. What if it was another one of those things? How could he be sure he had divine protection? One word, in Kester's voice, came into his head. '*Trust*'.

The atmosphere was definitely changing; Lucas felt whatever it was approaching him. And he knew there was more than one of them, he just knew it... He spun around, and the sight that greeted him made his jaw drop and a strangled sound escape from his mouth. Behind him, were two rows of monks. Hazy shadows, but definitely monks. He could make out their robes, and the fact their hands were pressed together as if in prayer. They were walking along the nave, with one monk at the head of the procession. As they drew nearer, the monk at the front stopped. He smiled at Lucas and nodded. He made the sign of the cross and Lucas blinked. When he opened his eyes again, they were gone. Lucas jumped to his feet and ran out of the Priory grounds. It was stupid, he knew. He wasn't scared of them – what was there to be scared of? But somehow felt he was intruding on something private and he had the strong sense that he shouldn't be there. *I've done my bit!* he felt like shouting. *It's up to you lot now!*

***

Lucas ran out of the Priory grounds and along the side streets towards the B&B. Normality. That's what he wanted. He'd had enough – more than enough – and couldn't wait to get back home. That was it though – today, they all left the Island and he would never have to come back again. He sprinted up the road and rounded the corner. A red mini was parked right outside of it, and a girl sat on the fence, cradling a mug of coffee. He started and stared at her. For a brief moment, he thought it was Cass. She flicked her straight, strawberry blonde hair over her shoulders and stared back at him.

'Laura?' he said.

'Why act so surprised?' she asked. She balanced the mug on the fencepost, jumped down and came over to him. 'I texted you. I told you. Don't make me wish I hadn't bothered.'

'I never got the message,' he said, 'there's no signal.'

'Hmmm,' said Laura. She'd piled on the mascara again, he noticed. God, he'd missed seeing that. Even down to the tiny smudges where her eyelashes had tickled her cheek when she blinked. 'The landlady's nice,' she said. 'She gave me toast. And coffee. They said you'd been at the Priory for some reason.' Lucas nodded. 'I just got here, really,' Laura continued. 'I had to wait to get across on the causeway. Drew's eating your breakfast, by the way. He said he'd waited long enough.'

'I didn't realise I'd been so long,' he said. 'I was just doing some research.' He paused. 'I'm so sorry. Sorry about everything.'

'Yeah, well. I'm not making any promises,' she said. 'I was up for my cousin's hen weekend. It wasn't that much further to come up here. I've never been before.' She looked around. 'It's nice isn't it? The landlady said you got stuck in the refuge hut overnight.' She grinned suddenly. 'Only you could do that - idiot.' She reached out and ruffled his hair. 'Still, at least you weren't messing with the island girls,' she said. 'Anyway. Like I said. No promises. I just don't know what to do. There's a tiny, tiny part of me,' she held up her hand and pinched her finger and thumb together, 'that thinks I don't want to let you go. There's a bigger, much bigger part,' she extended her arms as far as they would go, 'that says I should walk away.' She let her arms drop and looked at him. 'What's it to be?'

'The first one?' he asked.

'Well now. That's up to you, isn't it?' she replied.

'You're right,' said Lucas. 'I've got to make this bit,' he took hold of her hands and squeezed her thumb and forefinger together as she had done, 'into this bit.' He swung her arms apart and she laughed. The laughter sounded good. 'I'll do it Laura. I promise.' He became serious. 'You don't often get second chances. I appreciate it.'

Her arms were the perfect width apart now for him to move closer and wrap them behind his body. He was very pleased to feel her arms tighten around him. He had had more than a second chance, he realised, what with everything that had happened, but the bite marks might take some explaining away, if she ever got to the point where she might see them…but he would worry about that later. For the moment, though, he was happy. Laura seemed quite calm. She smelled of shower gel and perfume, and he held her close for a minute, breathing her in. Then he lowered his face to hers. He kissed her, and was very pleased to realise that she was kissing him back.

Epilogue

There is a famous quote that says, "time and tide wait for no-one". It's wrong. Something, somewhere controls the time and the tide. And when everything is in the perfect condition, and everything is where it should be, things can happen. Some people call it Fate. Others call it synchronicity. But whatever it is, it exists.

So, just after the sun had risen somewhere off the northern coast of Jura in the Southern Inner Hebrides, the tidal force of the *Coire Bhreacain* whirlpool smashed a silver dagger off the peak of the underwater mountain and sent it spinning through the waves. The dagger was carried along to the shore near Kinundrach and pitched up on the rocky coastline near Barnhill.

Katie Logan found it. She saw it lying on the rocks when the first rays of sunlight flashed off the diamonds embedded into the hilt. It made her stop in her tracks and distracted her from walking straight out into the roaring waves and never coming back. She bent over and picked it up, staring at it as if it was the most entrancing thing in the world. She felt her heart beat faster and then suddenly, she understood. She didn't know what the dagger was or what it meant, but she knew it was important. And she knew that she had been meant to find it.

The End

By the same author

THE MEMORY OF SNOW

Three eras.
Three young women.
Three Guardians, separated by centuries.

Aemelia: the Christian daughter of a Roman Commandant.

Meggie: accused of witchcraft in the seventeenth century.

Liv: a twenty-first century teenager, intent on finding information for a project.

When horrors from the past threaten her, Liv discovers she is a Guardian of the mystical Coventina's Well. She must work with the spirits who linger there, and use their combined power to banish evil from the sacred spring.

A paranormal novel, weaving together fact and fiction and set amongst the wild landscape of Hadrian's Wall in Northumberland, *The Memory of Snow* tells the story of the Guardians of Coventina's Well and how three young women from three different eras must confront both the tragic past and the potential future to help each other survive.

www.rosethornpress.co.uk

Printed in Great Britain
by Amazon.co.uk, Ltd.,
Marston Gate.